DEAD GAME

By Shirley Swift

Copyright © 2013 Eastwood Books
Shirley Swift & Ted Howe
ISBN-13: 978-1492970002
ISBN-10: 149297000X

To the 1942 Men's Basketball
State of Michigan Championship Team
from Decatur, Michigan High School:
Their team inspired this story although
names, dates, and other pertinent facts were
all changed ☺ Only the small town
spirit was captured for the story.

Thank you to my fine editors,
Stephen Tod and Joseph Higdon and
Richland Area Writers' Circle
for continued encouragement.

Deadly Game - Prologue

Bill shifted his weight uneasily in the car seat and tried to clear his mind. "Think -- do something," his mind raced. He was aware of the heat rising in his face as the driver named, with a cold satisfaction, the men that had been killed. Bill stared straight ahead, trying to appear unaffected by the driver's tale. It was all a game – a sick perversion. Had the other men panicked? Perhaps if he kept his cool he would not meet the same fate as the other victims of this deranged person, once a trusted friend.

The past events were all so clear now, that Bill almost laughed at the irony to have been correct about his other friends' "accidents." He had been suspicious for the past two years and kept records. Why hadn't he told anyone? Would anyone ever find the book? Would anyone care if … a surge of adrenalin shot through him as Bill remembered his partner, Summer. He would have to try to escape.

"You might as well accept it, Bill. You're not going anywhere. I've won."

"This is all just a game to you, isn't it? Bill's hands shook.

The psychotic driver just laughed. "Revenge is mine, sayeth the Lord!"

As the car slowed on the gravel road Bill decided to jump out and make a run for it. He managed to open the door, but the seat belt kept him from flinging himself to freedom. He unlatched the belt lock just as the driver slammed on the brakes, throwing Bill forward, causing him to hit his head against the dashboard. He turned, intent on overpowering his captor. He managed to grab the driver's hair, but was too disoriented to do any harm. His temples pounding, Bill heard the driver roar with laughter as the needle found its target.

The next morning Bill Bates did not open his book store. Two youngsters walking around Emerald Lake spied a body floating just off the southern shore.

The master of his personal sport sighed with contentment – another of Kensington's leading citizens had been eliminated from the deadly game.

HOME AGAIN – Chapter One

  Kensington, a sleepy village in southern Michigan, is situated on the eastern shore of Emerald Lake. A natural hilly region from the west creates a cove that juts out into the lake and the Emerald Harbor Inn overlooks the lake's activities from there.

  A resort is located to the north. A scouting camp and a church-run retreat for boys is to the south. Baker Park, within the village limits is near the Baker House, a small bed and breakfast. The park is used for family gatherings and is where the local gym teacher gives swimming lessons. The sheriff's water patrol office is also based at the park.

  The majority of inhabitants are farmers and the town's small business owners. Kensington swells to twice its population in the spring and summer months due to migrant families that live on area farms to tend and harvest vegetables and fruits. Tourists from Chicago and other near by towns flock to the region for the lake's crystal, spring-fed water's bass and blue-gill fishing as well as vacationing at the camps and the resort. The 20-year old sign at the village limit State "Class C" boys' basketball championship title.

  The sign also serves to remind long-time residents of the tragic car accident that killed one of the basketball players and injured three others the night after the tournament. Several of the team members had chosen to live in Kensington after school and college, including business owners and the sheriff. One of the injured team members, Bill Bates drowned on Thursday, the tenth of June, 2010.

  The news of Bill's body being discovered floating offshore of the Boys' Retreat camp weighed heavily with Bates' mother, Amanda, and sister, Kathryn. The women returned to their hometown, Kensington, the evening they received word of Bill's death. Through her shock, Kathryn, also known as Kit, had the gnawing feeling that something was wrong. Her brother was an excellent swimmer. It was just not possible he drowned.

While the women both lived in Lansing, they did not share Amanda's home. Even after Kit's husband, Gregg, died, Kit preferred staying in her two bedroom townhouse alone. However, at their return, they were sharing a suite in the Baker House Bed and Breakfast.

After unpacking, Kit opened a bottle of cherry brandy. "It was very kind for the minister to make all the arrangements for the funeral," Kit said.

Amanda nodded. After a short while she said, "Especially since we're not church members. I'm glad the funeral will be tomorrow so we don't have to stay long."

"I remember how difficult it was for you when I came here for the summers," Kit said. She poured a small amount of the brandy in their snifters.

Amanda nodded. "I didn't know you under-stood." She swirled the red liquid around and inhaled its fragrance.

Kit corked the bottle and curled up in the easy chair. Were those tears she saw in her mother's eyes? "I know," she answered quietly. Kensington holds sad memories for you, Mom."

Amanda leaned back on the sofa. She tasted the brandy and swished it around in her mouth. As she looked at the ceiling, tears flowed down her cheeks.

"Life is complicated, Mom."

Amanda swallowed the brandy and whispered, "Very." She wept openly.

Kit put her brandy down and moved to the sofa next to her mother. She put her arms about her shoulders. That brought on a deluge of tears from both women; each comforting the other.

Thursday morning, Kit looked out across Main Street. Amanda finished dressing. The morning sunrise was partially hidden by the dark clouds, creating an ominous gloom over the town. It was Kit's stereotypical day for a funeral – overcast. The frequent gusts of wind blew dust devils across the fields and into the streets, stirring up the remnants of last fall's dead leaves and the early summer's dried top soil. From experience, she knew the area farmers had been irrigating early in the year. Crops were already suffering. Townspeople were watering in hopes of saving lawns and shrubs.

The women went to the dining room for the complimentary breakfast. Rain, or lack thereof, was the major topic of discussion in the dining room.

The women heard a guest at a nearby table say, "There are reports of scattered showers."

"Believe it when I see it," commented his companion.

Kit picked at her food and stared out the side window. The Baker House's rotating sprinkler showered a corner of the glass from time to time.

Amanda leaned closer to Kit and half-whispered, "You know I'm rather glad it's not raining. The cemetery will be a washout if it does."

Kit was about to agree when she saw rain hitting against all of the windows. Turning to her mother with a smirk she said, "You might know it." Things surrounding her life hadn't been going right for quite a while. Why would the weather cooperate? The light shower became a downpour and while ignored by the B&B's guests, the waitress was joined by the cook from the kitchen to look outside. It lasted for about 15 minutes, and then a soft drizzle settled over the area. All the while the sprinkler pumped its precious water onto the lawn and down the side window.

By two o'clock when the funeral director picked up Amanda and Kit, the light rain had still not subsided. The driver very quickly opened an umbrella for them as they made their way to the limousine and then again from the limousine up the church steps. The women were greeted by old friends and townspeople they didn't know. Kit's stomach knotted when she saw Sheriff Tyler Stone come into the church. He had matured well, his sandy brown hair sun-streaked. She noted his air of confidence and was impressed how he looked so trim in his uniform. What an odd sensation, she thought. Wasn't she beyond reacting to him the way she had years ago?

The service began and Kit sighed heavily. Life was making her stronger, wasn't that what Nietzsche said? "That which doesn't kill you makes you stronger?" She longed to have someone else be strong for her – just for a short while. Her thoughts drifted to Tyler Stone again, and she shook it off. Kit took a deep breath, held it, and let it go slowly. She had learned to calm herself during her fourth grade students' insurrections by concentrating on her breathing. The funeral and seeing Tyler again upset her enough that she fell back on the breathing technique to once again think clearly. She was proud of her independence and wouldn't let thoughts of letting someone else take care of her get a toe-hold in her mind.

The minister was talking about Bill's spirituality being directly linked to his love of nature. Kit thought it appropriate that her brother's passing was being observed by Mother Nature herself. It was as though the old gal was opening the heavens because she was going to miss Bill's adoration of her beauty. Now, she would hold Bill in her bosom for all eternity. Her brother really had appreciated nature with the seasonal changes and the birds ... and what was the minister saying? Somehow Kit gathered herself and her thoughts as people began to pass by Bill's casket.

She noticed that, while paying their respects, the people didn't linger. A few just walked by without even looking at the casket. A couple went by and the woman made the sign of the cross while the man bowed his head. An older couple shuffled by, helped by a couple in their sixties. Kit knew them, but couldn't remember both of their names. His name, Gus, stuck with her for some reason. Perhaps he was a fishing buddy of her dad.

Kit and Amanda were the last to view the body. What an odd custom it is to look at the corpse, Kit thought. This wasn't her brother Bill. He was strong and full of life. He was the tease that pulled her hair. He was the proud winner of the swim across the lake when he was 15. Bill was the promising athlete that ended up limping from that accident after the basketball championship. He listened to Kit when she needed advice in college. He consoled her when she had lost Gregg. She would truly miss her brother.

They left the chapel and the funeral director closed the casket, forever shutting his body away from the world. It was time to go to the cemetery. Kit was relieved that at least it had stopped raining even though gardeners and farmers surrounding Kensington wished it had not.

A few men she knew served as pall bearers. She knew Bill was watching and laughing once again because of that old worn-out joke he often told about being a "polar bear." They rode in the limousine to the cemetery, both women dry-eyed.

On the way, Kit stared out the limo window, the country-side a blur. She thought of how they cried for hours together the night before; their empathy feeding on each other's emotions. They were both mourning Bill but Kit believed that each, in their own way, were digging into their unexpressed grief for losses that went back for years.

The funeral director's stopping the limousine brought Kit back to the present. He helped them out of the limo and led them to the freshly dug gravesite.

Most of those attending the service did not go to the cemetery. The remaining small gathering of mourners stood silently beneath the canopy erected for protection against the weather. Even though the rain had subsided just a short while ago, the sun had come out full force and the mid-afternoon humidity made the closeness nearly unbearable. Kit tried to concentrate on the Scripture being read and stared at the roses on the casket until they blurred. She closed her eyes to pray and tears spilled onto her cheeks. She hadn't been aware of crying again and wondered where the tears came from. It had been almost a year since she had seen Bill, heard his laughter. Had she told him she loved him when she last saw him?

Kit was angry with herself again because she realized that she was lost in her own thoughts when her brother was being laid to rest. By the time the minister concluded the ceremony she was fleeing the sickening sweet fragrance of the roses and lilies.

"Let her go," Sheriff Stone whispered to Amanda as he helped her to her feet. "She needs some time alone."

"Thank you, Tyler." Amanda Bates nodded as she took her young friend's arm. "This last year hasn't been easy on her; first Gregg's dying and now Bill." They walked toward the funeral director's limousine, and Amanda slid into the back seat. "Will you keep an eye on her, Tyler? I'm going back to the Baker House."

"Sure, I'll see to it she gets home." He smiled and tipped his hat. He watched her go and then walked to where Kit was leaning against a tree.

"Are you all right, Kathryn?" Tyler asked gently.

"Yes, Sheriff Stone." Kit turned to him, feeling that same tug in her mid-section. "I just felt so closed-in under the canvas. The smell of the flowers was overwhelming. I needed some fresh air."

They stood in silence and watched the few mourners leaving. A tall auburn-haired woman, dressed in a long flowing black dress, lingered behind. She placed a flower on the casket, bit her lip and looked toward Kit. With no sign of recognition she turned slowly and was gone. Kit could not place her. Obviously the woman had known her brother and was mourning as well. Was the woman reaching out to her? Kit was afraid to trust her emotions, let alone her intuition today. "Do you recognize that woman?"

Tyler turned to the gravesite. He realized he had been staring at Kathryn. "I'm sorry, I missed her." Kathryn Bates had always distracted him. She was the prettiest of all the girls that had been in his younger brother's high school class. Even when Tom had dated her years before Tyler couldn't help but admire her raven-colored hair and sparkling blue eyes. Now she had returned to Kensington a grown woman, more enchanting than Tyler Stone could have imagined.

Kit was amused by the sheriff's observation of her. "Well, I suppose we should leave."

"You're right, Kitty. Your mama asked me to see that you get back to the Baker House."

Kit smiled and shook her head. The sheriff and his younger brother were among the few people she knew that still called her by her childhood nickname. "As if I'd get lost in Kensington," she replied. Impulsively she reached out and grabbed his arm and squeezed it tightly. "You'd better see me to town then, Sheriff. No telling who is lurking behind these gravestones."

Tyler felt that Kathryn was trying to hide her grief by making light of her mother's concern. He walked her back to the squad car aware that his palms were sweating. Maybe if she had this kind of effect on him, he wasn't such a lost cause after all!

Riding in silence made Tyler uneasy. "Do you follow the Tigers?"

"Bill and I wrote about them. He was so upset when Galarraga was robbed of that perfect game last week that he phoned me."

Tyler grinned. "The umpire made a bad call. Hope they have a winning season this year."

"If Cabrera keeps hitting the way he is, they might."

"Verlander is coming up in the ranks."

"Yeah, Bill thinks he'll be around for a while. I mean 'thought.'

Tyler realized she used the present tense the same time Kit did.

"That was the last time I talked to him." Kit said quietly. They fell silent again.

As they arrived at the B & B's parking lot, Tyler shut off the motor and turned to Kit. "I'm truly sorry about Bill's passing, Kitty." When Kit looked at her hands and smiled he said, "Perhaps I should call you Kathryn."

"It doesn't matter, Sheriff."

Tyler just nodded and continued, "You know what good friends Bill and I were."

"I know you'll miss him. You also know what a good swimmer he was. There's something wrong about his death, Sheriff."

Tyler winced inside. He was not at all sure whether it was from her being so formal or from the statement she had made. "Accidents happen. We can't bring him back."

Kit understood accidents. She also understood people being gone forever. She also understood that some accidents are preventable. Kit swallowed the quick retort that was forming because she sensed the strain in his voice. Kit suddenly knew the sheriff had questioned the drowning also. "Did you investigate?" she asked.

"Yes," he interrupted, "Thoroughly. I couldn't find any sign that something other than an accidental drowning occurred."

Kit looked at her hands again, purposefully avoiding Tyler's eyes. "The lawyer is expediting the reading of my brother's will tomorrow. Mother is going home right after seeing him. But I'm going to stay long enough to close up the shop or tie up any other loose ends. Perhaps I can speak with you about what you learned from your investigation some other time. It's only been a few days." She met his eyes.

"That would be fine." He jumped at the chance to see her again and added cautiously, "but I doubt it will help. There's just nothing more to tell."

"Thanks for the ride." She smiled and Tyler quickly got out of the car and opened her door. She wanted to make a clever comment about men in his generation knowing how to treat a lady, but somehow he just didn't seem as old as she remembered him to have been.

"Tom will be home this evening. I'm sure he'll want to see you," Tyler said as he shut the door.

"I haven't seen him in years. How is he?"

Tyler walked her to the door. "Tom's doing well. He's a regional director of his sales firm now and is on the road a lot. Would you and your mother feel up to having dinner with us?"

"I'm sure it will be all right," she answered, flashing him a lovely smile.

"Pick you up at seven then," he managed, thinking his heart had skipped a beat.

Kit nodded and went in, leaving Tyler feeling on edge.

The sheriff drove back to the office still feeling edgy. It took him very little time to realize that it was his reaction to Kathryn making him that way. He thought he should have his head examined. What would people think, taking the women out to dinner? But Kathryn had said it would be okay and everyone knew they were from out of town. Why were appearances always so important to him?

Kit let herself into the suite.

Amanda was casually tossing her clothing into the suitcase which lay open on her bed. She stopped long enough to face Kit, observing that her daughter appeared to be in control of her emotions.

"Hi," Kit smiled. "I see you're getting ready to leave."

"Are you okay?" Amanda asked as she turned back to the packing.

"As good as can be expected, Mom. In fact, I accepted a dinner invitation for us tonight."

"You did? With whom?"

"Tyler & Tommie Stone."

"Oh, they'll be good company."

"Why did you want the sheriff to watch over me, Mom?"

"I was concerned Bill's funeral would, uh ..."

"... remind me of Gregg," Kit finished quietly.

"Yes."

"There isn't a day that goes by that I don't think of him, want him back. It's been almost eight months since Gregg died and I know that I have to go on. Bill's death just adds to the losses I've had. I loved them both so much."

"You probably think I'm terribly callous about Bill. I have been grieving our estrangement for years, you know. Still, he was my son and I loved him dearly. I just don't show it."

"I understand, Mom." Kit gave her a warm hug. Bill had chosen to live with his dad in Kensington after her parents' divorce and Amanda didn't quite get over that.

"I still intend to ask Tyler to take care of you while you're here, Kit."

"Mom, I'm a big girl now and quite capable of taking care of myself. Are you all packed?" she asked, changing the subject.

"Except for what I'll wear to the lawyer's office. I'll finish everything else in the morning," she answered.

Kit decided to take a quick shower and found her mother's cosmetics strewn about the sink. A wet towel was draped over the back of the stool and a pair of pantyhose was hanging on the shower rod. She chuckled to herself at her mother's chaos; she had often wondered if that had been one of her parents' problems. As she showered she thought of summers spent in Kensington with her father and brother and her appreciation for their neatness and order.

Kit's father had died several years before and had not known her husband, Gregg. Her brother, Bill, and Gregg had become friends and enjoyed fishing together. Kit remembered hearing the men's laughter across the lake as they sat in the boat off shore. Their lively discussions around the dinner table about the NBA and the Detroit Tigers made her warm inside. She cherished her memories of their times together.

Kit finally allowed tears to flow as the hot water beat upon her head. She was angry and hurt that she had been deserted by all of the men in her life; first her father, then her husband Gregg, and now her brother.

Kit toweled dry and she told herself, for probably the hundredth time, that death is not desertion. It is part of life – a journey to another plane of existence. It simply was her father's and husband's time.

Her father died of stomach cancer. The suffering had been bad at the end and Kit was relieved for his passing. Gregg died because of an accident. Although he was young, Kit dealt with the fact that his accident had not been avoided.

However, she didn't believe for one minute that it was Bill's "time." It was simple reasoning – he could not have drowned.

Kit emerged from her room to see that Amanda was wearing a gray wide-legged pair of flannel pants with a cream-colored top. A scarf around her neck surrounded her with streaks of gray and cream and red. Her silver hair was ever so curly and just the right length to show off the bright red earrings that swayed as she walked. As usual, she looked fabulous and somewhat exotic. It always amazed the younger woman that even though she thought her mother threw together an outfit rather haphazardly, she always looked great.

Kit just did not have the same flair as her mother and had chosen a blue tailored suit with matching shoes. Even with their style differences, they painted an enchanting picture of mother and daughter. They were ready on time and on the porch by seven.

Tyler Stone's deep voice interrupted Kit's thoughts, "Good evening, ladies."

"Tyler, I'm so glad you thought of this," Amanda bubbled and took his arm. Tom walked forward at that point and nodded to Kit.

"Hello, Kitty," he smiled, revealing his beautiful white teeth.

"Hi Tommie!" Kit returned his smile and then giggled at the face he made when she called him by his childhood name.

Amanda pretended to be angry and said, "You two kids get along now." Tyler just shook his head and led her out to the car.

"You sure have grown up," Tom whispered as his eyes roamed upwards slowly from her legs and then rested on her face.

Kit flushed and answered, "So have you. I hardly knew you without the metal grin."

"Score one for the teacher," Tom grinned sarcastically and was satisfied that it would be an amusing challenge to try to get Kit into his bed.

Amanda rode in the front seat of the LeBaron with Tyler, making it necessary for Kit to sit in the back with Tom. He casually put his arm about Kit's shoulders even though it made her uneasy. Kit noticed Tyler looking in the rear view mirror at them. Tom also saw his big brother looking, and he chuckled under his breath.

They drove the few miles out to the Emerald Harbor Inn. The Inn catered to several surrounding towns and during this summer season was highly patronized by locals and tourists as a place of fine dining.

All remnants of rain were gone, and a soft breeze had blown the humidity away. Since the night was warm, they opted to eat out on the terrace overlooking Emerald Lake. Kit wondered if anyone gave any thought to the fact that this was the same lake where her brother had drowned. She stood at the deck railing watching the fireflies over the water until Tom took her elbow and nodded toward the table.

Tyler picked up the wine list. "They have some outstanding local wines here."

Tom asked Kit, "Do you like good dry merlot?" as they sat down.

"Not particularly. If I'm going to have sugar, I'd rather taste it," she smiled.

Tom screwed up his face, "Well, you'll just have to taste their merlot here."

Amanda looked at Tyler, "What would you suggest?"

"Since I am driving, I will limit myself to one excellent white – their Blue Heron."

"Having fish again, I suppose." Tom shook his head. He turned to Kit, "You've got to have their filet mignon, and that requires merlot!"

"I'd rather have their stuffed squab," Kit answered. "And I'll taste both wines!"

Kit ordered the stuffed squab. Amanda ordered their lemon-crusted white fish with rice pilaf as did Tyler. Tom, of course, had the filet mignon. Dinner talk turned toward the early dry spell they were having. "The farmers are concerned about a drought this year," Tyler began.

"No matter where I travel in this area, it's the same," Tom added. "About thirty miles east of here, however, they have some flooding."

Well, they could agree about something, Kit thought as the men continued comparing the climate conditions throughout eating their salads. She was beginning to think that there was a problem between the brothers other than what remained from their earlier sibling rivalry.

Tom paid far too much attention to Kit, and it made her uncomfortable. He seemed to be forcing his hand with her – first the wine, then the menu. He seemed to be staking his territory because he was interested in her romantically. As long as she was staying in Kensington for a while, she would have to let him know she was not interested in romance.

The meals arrived and Amanda said they were prepared with elegance. "What a lovely presentation."

Tom shook his head disapprovingly when Kit's squab arrived. "You really should have tried this filet mignon. Red meat protein gives one plenty of energy." He smiled lasciviously at Kit.

Amanda saw the tension building and sought to change the subject. "So, Tyler, I trust there are no crime sprees in Kensington."

Before he could answer, Tom commented, "Well, there is a drug problem that our police force has not been able to curb."

"In Kensington?" Kit asked surprised.

"There is a problem," Tyler began. "Hopefully, by the Fourth, we'll be in control."

"Imagine that," Amanda commented.

"Imagine that," Tom repeated sarcastically and grinned at Tyler.

Kit hurriedly asked, "Do they still have fire-works on the Fourth?"

Tyler was glad for the change of subject. "Yes, we go out on the lake ..."

Kit only half heard what he was saying. She looked over the balcony. The lake glistened in the moonlight. Occasionally some Canadian geese that decided to nest there called to one another. A place that once had been so beautiful to her now was overshadowed by her building theory of Bill's murder.

A carafe of coffee had been delivered to their table. "How long will you be in Kensington, Kit?" Tom asked her as he poured her a cup. He pressed his knee against hers.

Unflinchingly, she moved her leg away, took the coffee, and answered, "Until I find my brother's killer."

Tom's steely gray eyes returned her stare. He said flatly, "Bill's death was an accident."

"Kathryn, whatever are you talking about?" her mother asked.

Kit turned to her mother and almost giggled; the shock was so apparent on her mother's face. But Kit quickly sobered. "I told you, I just can't accept that Bill drowned accidentally." Kit noted that Tyler's face did not hide his surprise at her statement either.

Tom reached over and enfolded her hand in his. "I'll help you any way I can, Kit."

"Thank you, Tom." She turned to the sheriff then. "May I come to your office tomorrow, Sheriff?"

"Certainly," Tyler answered. He wondered if Kit's suspicions were her way of coping with her brother's death.

"Well, I don't want to be a wet blanket, but we have an early appointment at the lawyer. Then, I have to catch the bus," Amanda said.

"Ty can drop us off at the local pub," Tom said to Kit. "I'll see you home a while later. We have a lot of catching up to do," he smiled.

"Thank you, dear friend, but I'm beat. I need some sleep," Kit responded warmly and rose from the table. Tom turned toward the lake but not before Kit saw that he was frowning.

The men saw them back to the Baker House, with Tyler once again being a gentleman and getting the door for Amanda. He also opened the back door for Kit before Tom got to the other side of the car. Amanda turned and gave Tom a peck on the cheek. "It was wonderful to see you again, Tom." She took Tyler's arm and walked toward the B & B's porch.

"Well, I don't have to leave town for a few days. What time can we get together tomorrow?" Tom pulled Kit toward him.

Kit ached with the feel of his lean body against her. She backed away from him gently but firmly. "I need a friend, Tom – nothing more. If you don't respect that, we won't see each other while I'm here."

"Okay, little Kitty. You win. I'm going to give you some friendly advice then. Drop this thing about your brother. It won't serve any purpose but make you more withdrawn and depressed."

"Withdrawn?"

Tom broke into a condescending smile, only slightly showing his straightened teeth – his silence saying more than an explanation. Kit had the urge to put her fist through those teeth. "Goodnight. Dinner was pleasant." She turned on her heel, leaving the younger Stone alone in the parking lot.

Tyler passed her in the lobby as she came in alone. "Good night, Kathryn," he nodded. It looked like Tom struck out.

"Good night, Tyler. Thank you for dinner. I enjoyed it. I'll see you tomorrow after Mom leaves."

"It was my pleasure," Tyler answered and Kit had the notion that he really meant it.

The men drove off in silence. As they neared the home they shared, Tom asked, "What do you think is in that pretty little head of hers to think Bill was murdered?"

Tyler didn't miss his brother's description of Kit. "I'm not sure. I know she's still grieving for her husband and now this with her brother … "

" … is probably just too much for her," Tom interrupted. "I'll make sure to give her extra attention while she's here." Tom knew that was a calculated blow to Tyler's ego. He saw his older brother's muscles in his jaw clenching. Yes, making a play for Kit would be amusing.

Amanda was in bed already, her clothes thrown over the back of the chair. "That was interesting, wasn't it?"

"You mean watching those two spar?" said Kit.

"There was always a competitive spirit between the two of them as they grew up."

"You'd think they would have outgrown it by now, but I don't think Tyler feeds into it like Tom seems to."

"Very observant, my child. The good sheriff and his little brother appear to both want your attention. It's just that Tom is more aggressive."

"You're a good judge of character, Mom. It does explain why Tom is coming on to me."

"Ego. One-up-man-ship. Lust."

"Mom." Kit laughed.

"The wine has definitely gone to my sleep center and I am about to crash. Good night!" Amanda trailed off and was asleep in minutes.

Kit sat in the window seat, staring across the street. The past crowded in on her, and she let her mind wander to re-direct her thoughts. Tom was her age, almost black hair, square jaw, always a five-o'clock shadow and dark gray brooding eyes. He resembled his father as Kit remembered him. He was full of quick energy and reacted in anger a great deal, while Tyler took his time to weigh situations and was easy going. Tyler was taller by a good two inches and that always seemed to have made little Tommie jealous. He also had sandy-colored hair that showed red highlights in the sun and had beautiful deep blue eyes ... just like his mother. Their brother, Mike, was more like Tommie and their father. Kit decided she liked Tyler's moustache and how he looked in the sheriff's uniform. The white at his temples was very attractive, also. She moved from the window seat to her bed and clutched her pillow. Soon her thoughts of the Stone brothers dissolved and she was lulled to sleep by her mother's breathing.

In the morning the women ate breakfast in the Baker House dining room and walked over to the lawyer's office. "Henry James, Esq. – Attorney at Law," read Amanda aloud.

"Esquire." Kit smiled. "Interesting that Bill, seller of books would have a friend with the name of a literary giant."

"Doubt there's any family connection."

Kit didn't answer. Henry opened the door for them. "Good morning, ladies."

"Hello, Henry," Amanda smiled. "Thank you for meeting with us on a Saturday."

Kit nodded to him. "We appreciate your expediting this reading. With our living out of town it helps a great deal."

"My pleasure to help. Have a seat please." Henry motioned to a set of chairs opposite his large oak desk. He sat down and opened a manila folder.

"Bill made this will out in April of 2005. He had an appointment to see me after the July holiday. He was going to update it."

"Oh. I'm sorry to hear that," Kit said.

Amanda bit her lower lip. "Do you have any idea of what he intended to do?"

Henry answered, "No. This is his last will and testament and it stands as is. I can read it all or just abbreviate it."

"Please abbreviate it, Henry," Amanda said.

"The will was signed before me on April 5, 2008. All of his worldly goods, including his store, Bates' Books, his personal items, his bank accounts, and shares in various local businesses all are bequeathed to his sister, Kathryn Bates Anderson, of Lansing, Michigan.

"Exceptions are: (1) to his mother, Amanda Bates, he bequeaths family heirlooms of her choice, to be determined by mutual consent with Kathryn Bates Anderson, and the books he owns of Amanda's favorite poet. (2) to his best friend, Tyler Stone, he bequeaths his fishing and angling gear.

"And that is the abbreviated form, ladies."

"Thank you, Henry. Is there anything for me to sign?" asked Amanda.

Henry produced a statement for Amanda's signature. Then he passed it to Kit for her signature. The women stood up, shook his hand, and thanked him once again.

"I will be in touch with you, Mrs. Anderson, as soon as the deeds are filed."

"Thank you, Henry, and please call me Kathryn."

The women walked back to the Baker House. The day was warm already and Kit noted some places had their water sprinklers on.

Amanda brought Kit back to reality. "When do you have to be back to your job?"

"I don't have to report until mid-August so I'll have the entire summer to get the book shop ready to be sold."

"Are you sure?"

"Yes, I want to do this. I need to do this."

"I understand. Don't get too caught up with the Stone brothers' feuding."

Kit looked up at her mother and saw the huge smile. "They're quite a pair, aren't they?" They laughed together.

"You know you really surprised me last night when you said Bill had been murdered."

"Yes. I know. It's a gut feeling because he hadn't said anything about his heart being a problem and you know how well he could swim."

"Time has a way of changing things for all of us, Kit."

"Bill wasn't even 40, Mother."

"I know." She looked at her wrist watch. "I'd better get going."

Kit went to the bus depot with her mother. "I'll send you a box of clothing as soon as I can," Amanda said.

"Thanks, Mom. I don't need very much for the summer."

"I'll do my best." Amanda waved from the bus window, and Kit blew her a kiss. Tyler was also there to see Amanda off. He and Kit stood on the sidewalk in silence as the bus pulled away and then Kit decided she would declare her independence.

"Sheriff," she began. "I am going to need your help but I don't want to be the object of your every concern. I'm a grown woman and I don't need protection. I promise I won't be a pest. Do we have a deal?"

"One condition – stop calling me 'Sheriff'. You make me feel ancient."

Kit let out a surprised giggle. "Why, Tyler Stone, you're in great shape!" She took an appreciative glance over him, thus re-confirming what she had noticed the day before. She reached up and touched the white at his hairline and added jokingly, "... not a day over 70!" He caught her hand, intending to kiss it but she drew it away laughing. It was contagious and the two of them laughed together walking toward his office. Neither of them missed that it turned a few heads.

Kit spent a few hours going over the initial report of her brother's drowning and then over the coroner's report as well. Tyler had business to take care of, so she was alone during that time. He returned to find her still concentrating on the file.

To Kit's knowledge, her brother had never had heart problems, but the report stated that Bill Bates had suffered a massive heart attack, thus causing him not to be able to swim. There was a large bump on his forehead, presumed to have been received when he fell over the side of the boat.

"How about some lunch?" he offered.

Kit jumped slightly and then visibly relaxed as she recognized Tyler.

"Sorry, I didn't mean to startle you." He smiled the same wide smile Tom had greeted her with the previous evening. She had noted their similar characteristics before. Only now, after her late night musings, she was becoming aware of their differences as well. Tyler truly did have an easy-going gentleness that Tom had not acquired.

"I'd really like to go to the book store, Tyler."

He went to his desk and opened a side drawer. "Here are the keys, Kathryn. I'll walk you there."

"No," she said. "I'd like to go alone." She snatched the keys from him. He nodded knowingly and she smiled. "Thanks anyway."

Kit's pace quickened as she neared her brother's book store. She realized her steps were matching the racing tempo her heart was beating out. A few doors away from her destination she encountered a small storefront with a sign that read "The Mystic Spinner." She had not seen the shop there a year ago when she had visited Kensington. Wanting to calm down before she went to the book store, she stopped to look at the window display. To her surprise, the mysterious auburn-haired woman from the funeral was inside.

The store owner looked up and nodded.

Curiosity got the best of Kit so she entered the shop. The breeze caused by the opening door made several nearby wind chimes ring. The sweet scent of sandalwood enveloped her, taking her back to a time not too far distant – to Gregg.

There were crystals in a glass case and some hanging prisms. She admired the colorful rainbows they created on the wall as the sun shone in on them. There were other stones, crystal orbs, gemstone jewelry, and a section of beads and beading materials. Kit wandered to the far side of the shop and saw tarot cards, Native American totems, flutes and a display of music CDs and tapes. A recording of a soulful melodic flute played in the background. She tried to concentrate on the shop's offerings, felt as though the woman behind the counter was watching her, so she looked up and smiled half-heartedly at her. The woman nodded. Marble containers held incense wands and the table had incense burners of every sort. Then, she spotted the smoke spiraling upwards from one of the incense burners. Once again, she was transported to the warm summer nights in Gregg's arms.

"Remembering?" the shop keeper asked softly. She had come from behind the counter and was just to Kit's side.

Still looking at the tiny stream of incense smoke, Kit shook her head "yes" and swallowed hard. "My husband."

"I've been told the pain will go away," the woman offered.

How could this stranger even guess what Kit was feeling, unless ... She turned and looked directly at her and was met with dark, piercing eyes. The woman smiled, softening her entire countenance, and Kit smiled in return. "You seem to speak from experience."

"Of course. Women like us have had our share of disappointments and pain with life and the men we have loved."

Kit couldn't resist asking, "Women like us?" She wanted to know if she was understanding her correctly.

The shop owner's smile faded and her crystal earrings flashed as she lifted her chin slightly. "Spiritually sensitive."

Kit smiled. "I believe I have found a much-needed friend. I'm Kathryn Anderson."

"Bill Bates' sister," the woman added and extended her hand. "I'm Summer Moon." Several bracelets jangled on Summer's arm as Kit shook her hand.

"I saw you at the funeral," Kit said.

The phone rang. "Excuse me." Summer turned away. "I have been waiting for this call."

There were tears in her eyes, Kit observed. She waited until Summer looked up and Kit mouthed, "I have to leave."

Summer covered the mouthpiece and said, "I'll talk with you again soon."

Kit stepped out into the sunlight knowing that she really had to get on with the task at hand. Bates' Books was five storefronts away. She nodded to the owner of the tobacco shop that was next to the book store. She remembered him as quiet, yet friendly over the years. Kit approached the book store, once again apprehensive.

In a few moments, she was there looking through the darkened windows at the displays. It took her a while to unlock the door as her hands were trembling so badly. She stumbled over the news-papers and envelopes that had piled up beneath the mail slot. She knelt to pick them up as the aroma of the old books overwhelmed her. Summers past and the good times she had had with her father and brother came rushing back. Wasn't it just yesterday that she had to stand on the stool to re-shelve books? And it couldn't have been years ago that she and Bill played hide-and-seek between the stacks and tables.

Kit sat down heavily on the floor and leaned against the door. Clutching a few of the envelopes, she wept. How she missed them! She had learned a great deal from her father and attributed her tenacity to him. He was warm and witty and shared his vast knowledge of books and authors with both her, and Bill, instilled a love of the out of doors as well.

The nights, after dinner, that her father read aloud to them as they sat in the glider on the back landing gave her a love for adventure books. Her dad would read "Nancy Drew" mysteries and then the "Hardy Boys" adventures. Even as children she and Bill speculated how the stories would end. Kit smiled as she thought of how her dad would change his voice as the Agatha Christie characters came alive on that back landing. It was all gone except for the memories.

After she calmed down, she scooped up the remaining items and deposited them on the counter. She found a tissue box and wiped the mascara streaks from her cheeks. She dreaded going into the back part of the store – her brother's office and then to the upper part of the building, his living quarters. That was part of her mission, however, to tie up loose strings and ready the store for sale.

Her brother's brown and white sweater was draped on the back of the swivel chair and it brought another wave of tears. She sat in the chair and wrapped the arms of the sweater about her and concentrated on her breathing until she calmed herself. She decided to tend to the paper work first. She called the newspaper office, making sure the subscription and the store's weekly advertisement was cancelled and then stacked the papers aside. Kit knew the account of Bill's "accident" was in the newspaper and she would read it later. It was probably much like the police report.

Sorting through the envelopes was fairly easy, and within a few minutes only a plain envelope remained. Without thinking she tore it open and read the warning note before it registered. "Miss Bates, Go home before you are hurt."

Kit stared at the note, anger welling up as she read it again. She had been right! She found the sheriff's phone number and was soon speaking with Tyler.

"Tyler, this is Kit. I just found a threatening note!"

"Are you sure?" he answered.

"Of course I'm sure," she almost shouted. "I told you there's more going on than meets the eye."

"Calm down, Kathryn, I'll be right over."

"Thanks, Tyler," she answered and hung up the phone. Kit read the short note again.

The bell on the front door tinkled, and Kit rose from the desk and met Tyler with a scowl. "Look at this, Tyler." She shook the note in the air. "Who would send this?"

Tyler could hardly suppress a smile. While he knew she was upset, he was amused how childlike she looked when angry. He almost thought she would pout and stamp her foot any moment.

"Sheriff Stone, I find this less than amusing."

Tyler took the note and hastily read it. "The person may have been concerned about your feelings."

"Hurt feelings? I don't buy that. Who would send this?"

"Well, any finger prints are certainly smudged. I suggest you keep this to yourself. I don't want a bunch of bounty hunters converging on Kensington." He reached into his shirt pocket and produced a business card. He scribbled on the back side. Here is my home phone number."

"Thanks," she answered and took his card and the threatening note from him.

"Well, I'll drive you to the Baker House if you're ready to leave now."

"No, thank you. I have a lot more to do here than I had thought. In fact, I think I'll move in here while I sort and clean for the sale."

Tyler noted the chill in Kit's voice and thought better of questioning her idea. He looked around and then said "I'd be glad to help."

Kit crumpled the mysterious note and tossed it into the waste can. "I can manage. I'd like to be alone now, if you don't mind." She faced Tyler in stony silence.

Tyler nodded. "Okay. Call if you need anything." He left realizing that she was upset with him for not having taken the note seriously. "Tyler" had come to her rescue but it was definitely "Sheriff Stone" that left the store.

Kit was angry. She thought Tyler had taken the threat much too lightly. As she tried to muddle through the accounting books, she kept second-guessing Tyler's attitude until by late afternoon she had talked herself into believing he was hiding the truth of her brother's death from her. The big question was why.

Tom was just leaving the B&B when Kit returned late that afternoon. "Just the person I was looking for!" he smiled broadly.

"Hello, Tom," she smiled wearily.

"Looks like you could use some company. How about dinner?"

"I'm a wreck. Quite frankly, I just need a long soak in a hot tub."

"You go soak and leave the rest to me. There's a great Chinese place a few blocks from here. I'll walk over and bring back dinner in a half-hour."

Kit was too tired to protest his extra effort, and she was hungry. "I'd appreciate that."

Tom winked and was gone. She went to the desk for her key and was soon in her room. Flowers had been sent the day before, but she noticed two more arrangements on the coffee table. Fifteen minutes later, she was bathed and dressed in a jogging outfit. Her brother's church had sent a lovely arrangement of daisies and carnations. The other was an unusual black orchid surrounded by thorny palm leaves. She was still looking for a card when Tom knocked at her door.

"It's me, Kitty! I'm back with dinner. The egg rolls await you!"

Kit let him in. Tom spread the dinner out on the coffee table with great flourish and began eating as Kit sat down. "I remember the first time we ate Chinese together. You speared the chicken with your chopsticks," she giggled.

Tom deftly picked up bean sprouts and rice with the slender tools. "Practice makes perfect," he replied and popped the food into his mouth with no difficulty.

Kit chose an egg roll as Tom put down the chopsticks and took a drink of tea. "Face it, Kathryn, we've come a long way from Cherry Cokes and marshmallows around a campfire. We had some good times, but it is the present I am interested in." He grinned and slid his arm toward her on the back of the couch and leaned closer.

"One has to bury the past completely to be able to be free to live in the present," Kit responded curtly, wondering why he had called her Kathryn.

A cloud seemed to descend on Tom, and he withdrew his arm. "Yes, burying the past is important. There is a lot of pain associated with the past, like my brother, Mike."

"You were very close to him. His death must have been hard to overcome."

"Yes. I'm still working on it. What about you and your husband?"

Kit sighed. "Gregg and I had an interesting life together. From the time we met until his death was less than three years. I can finally live for a few hours without thinking about him, and then something brings back a flood of memories. I smelled sandalwood incense burning this afternoon and it reminded me of Gregg."

"Sandalwood incense?" Tom asked.

"Yes, I discovered a delightful new age shop right here in Kensington run by a …"

"Red-haired witch," Tom interrupted. "She gives me the creeps."

Kit stared in disbelief. "Pardon me?"

"Summer Moon, your brother's woman."

"Oh, my goodness," Kit blurted out in surprise. It all made sense to her now.

"It'd be better if you stay away from that one," Tom continued.

Kit smiled weakly and fell silent. She had no intention of discussing Summer Moon with Tom. There had been a connection with her and she had to investigate further. Now that she understood Summer's connection with Bill, she was more determined to talk with the mysterious woman again soon.

Tom could see Kit was beginning to distance herself. "Looks like the old home town folk remembered you," Tom offered, referring to the flowers.

"Yes, most everyone has been very kind. This came today while I was out and I've not found a card," Kit said holding up the orchid.

"Let me see," Tom reached for the flower and closed his hands over hers. He looked deeply into her eyes and she felt her cheeks flushing. Tom knew she was lonely and Kit was not sure if she should be angry for his wanting to take advantage of her situation or flattered that he still found her attractive.

Kit dropped her eyes to the flower and spied a rolled piece of paper. "There it is." She took the vase from Tom and put it down on the coffee table. "Ouch! The palm bit me!" she giggled and withdrew her hand.

"You're bleeding," Tom said surprised. "What kind of a gift is this?"

Kit sobered suddenly and wrapped her finger in a napkin from the Chinese restaurant. "Perhaps, it's a warning too."

"Warning?" Tom asked. He used the chop sticks to remove the paper.

Kit didn't answer but unrolled the note. She paled as she read it. "Go home before you end up like your brother."

"Kitty, what is it?" Tom took the note and read it. "Tell me what's going on."

"It appears my brother's murderer is trying to tell me something." She took a deep breath and expected the same condescending attitude that his older brother had displayed earlier. Instead she saw Tom's jaw set in a tight line.

"You may be right," he managed.

For the first time Kit was really frightened. It would have almost been a relief for Tom to have laughed the threat away, but his agreement just confirmed what she had felt from the beginning. "Someone really did kill my brother," she barely breathed.

"I think it'd be a good idea to speak to Tyler about this," Tom remarked and moved toward the phone.

"No!" Kit answered quickly. "I've already discussed the subject with him, and I'm afraid he thinks I'm over-reacting to some well-meaning old lady."

"Did he say that?" Tom asked surprised.

Kit flushed. "Well, no, not exactly. But, he dismissed the other note as friendly."

"Other note?"

"Yes, there was an envelope left for me at the book store."

"Let me see it, Kit."

"I threw it away. Do you think there's something to all of this?"

Tom took Kit's hands in his. "Kit, dear, I don't want to see you upset, but you really could be in danger."

"Last night you said you'd help me, Tom. We'll have to start investigating."

"Not so fast. Now that someone is contacting you, it seems you should heed their warnings. I can make the necessary travel arrangements for you."

Kit withdrew her hands roughly. "You don't understand. I'm going to find my brother's killer. Are you willing to help or not?"

Tom shook his head slowly as he stared at the ceiling. He sighed deeply and answered, "What can I do?"

"First, I don't want Tyler to know about this."

"Agreed."

"Second, I'm going to move into the book store apartment." Kit smiled at Tom's shocked look. "Don't worry,

I'll be careful. I'll need you to do some checking around for me."

"Okay. I'll start with the florist. Perhaps that will give us a lead."

"Great idea!" Kit's eyes sparkled.

Tom pulled her into his arms and laughed. "That's more like my Kitty!" He brushed back a lock of her hair, "So beautiful and alive." He sought her lips.

Kit was swept up in the moment and responded to his kiss, warmed by the security his embrace offered. She had denied herself male attention for a long while even though there had been other opportunities. She enjoyed the hard muscling of Tom's body and the roughness of his kisses. Suddenly memories of Gregg flooded her, and the building passion was lost. She pulled away trembling. "I'm sorry, it's just too soon."

Tom pulled her close again and whispered huskily, "It's been too long."

Tears streamed from her eyes as she remembered the love shared with Gregg and knew these minutes with Tom had nothing to do with love. "Please, Tom. Things are bad enough."

Tom let go of her abruptly and stood up. "Perhaps you need someone less demanding, like my older brother."

Kit covered her eyes with her hands and began crying.

Tom cleared his throat. "Sorry, Kitty. I guess you're not ready for a man yet. I'd better leave." He turned toward the door.

Kit looked up fearfully. "Are you still going to help me?"

"Yes. I'll talk with you in a couple of days. I have a sales meeting in Ohio. I'll let you know what the florist says when I get back."

Kit smiled weakly, "Thanks."

He winked at her. "We'll get through this together."

Kit wept for a while after he left. Things were so confusing. One minute Tom was loving and the next ugly.

She and Gregg had never fought about sex so playing romantic games was not her style. She went to the bathroom, wet a washcloth and pressed it to her eyes, hoping they wouldn't swell. She went back out to the sofa and wondered why Tom said his brother would be less demanding of her. What was that supposed to mean? Certainly the sheriff was not interested in her; and yet, he had asked not to be called "sheriff."

The thought of being in Tyler Stone's arms made her flush – he was only eight years older than she! He had represented security to her until his passing off the threatening note as nothing. Now she was uncertain of even trusting him.

Kit decided not to even try to figure out the Stone men. She called the desk to arrange to check out in the morning and then packed her things.

Her awareness that her emotions were riding a rollercoaster didn't help. Trying to organize thoughts just made her toss and turn half the night. She spent the other half in nightmares of being in a fish tank and having a large fish chase her.

Tom had driven home practicing what he would say to Tyler. He had hoped to spend the night with Kit, just so his older brother would understand that he did not have a chance with the younger woman.

Tyler was pouring a cup of coffee when Tom let himself into the kitchen. "How's Kit tonight?" he asked, unable to hide his satisfaction that Tom had returned early. He went in the other room and sat in his easy chair.

Tom did not miss Tyler's reaction. "She's just fine, now. She was pretty upset over that note she got this afternoon." He turned his back to his brother and poured some coffee for himself. "It's a good thing I was around to comfort her. Yep, I'd say she's much better now."

Had Tyler seen Tom's face, he would have seen the mocking smile. Instead, he buried himself behind the paper and just grunted, "Good."

"If I were you, Ty, I'd try to get her to forget this hair-brained idea of finding Bill's supposed killer. I'm sure she'll listen to someone older and wiser, like you." Tyler only nodded. Tom chuckled to himself all the way to his room. Kit was attractive; however his interest in her was only as a challenge. He knew Tyler adored her, and the real prize was to make sure his older brother lost.

Tyler fumed as he read and re-read an advertisement about dog grooming. The words disappeared and all he could see was Kit in Tom's arms. He slammed the newspaper down and swore. He was being foolish. From somewhere deep within, he heard Kit's laughter. He was only eight years older than she – thirty-eight, did that really matter to her?

Sunday morning, 10 a.m., the cabbie deposited Kit and her suitcases in front of the book store. She was unlocking the door when a station wagon stopped at the curb. Kit recognized the older couple from her brother's church and nodded to them as they got out.

"Good morning, dear," Mrs. Walden chirped. "Could you use some help? Tom Stone called earlier and told us you would be moving in."

"How thoughtful of him," Kit replied. "I'd appreciate your help, Mrs. Walden."

"Oh, please, call us Elly," the older woman began.

"And Gus," her husband chimed in.

Gus Walden carried the suitcases in, and the women went upstairs into the apartment. Kit caught the lingering scent of sandalwood and smiled, realizing that Summer had been here with Bill.

They opened windows, allowing the rooms to be filled with warmth and sunshine. "Ah, fresh air!" smiled Elly.

Kit opened the closet doors, revealing the neatly arranged shirts, trousers and jackets. "I'm not sure what I should do with all of these," Kit sighed.

"We brought several boxes. Would you like for Gus and me to handle it? We'll pack things and you can decide if you want them stored or given to the needy."

Kit nodded. As if on cue, Gus entered the bedroom carrying the boxes. The three of them packed Bill's clothes and shoes. "I'm going to keep these two sweaters and this flannel shirt."

Elly just looked without saying anything.

"I might need them until Mom sends more of my clothes from home."

Elly had also brought a home-baked coffee cake so Kit made tea when they took a break. Kit had discovered her brother's cupboard well-stocked with herbal teas; and she couldn't help but think that, too, was Summer's influence. By eleven a.m. all was ready for Kit.

Elly had not stopped talking the entire time they were together. She helped Kit smooth the coverlet on the bed and stood back admiring the results of their labor. "There now," she smiled. "Clean as a whistle, dear. We'll be going now. Feel free to call us if you need anything -- number's in the phone book."

"Hope to see you at church next week," Gus added.

Kit thanked them again. Elly also had gathered the soiled laundry and promised to return the linens in a few days. So, she knew she would be in touch with them again, but didn't promise anything about Sunday. Then she realized they had given up their church service to help her. She made a mental note to thank them again.

It took her only a half-hour to put her clothes and toiletries away. Kit would have to do some clothes shopping until her Mom sent things.

She checked the locks on the back door. The landing still held the old slider. It now sported several pillows, and a small table to one side held a fern. Other hanging plants, hooked to the roofline had ivy and geraniums and cascading petunias. Summer's influence, no doubt.

Kit strained to look into the corners of the alley below. It was still private. She went downstairs to the street entrance and made sure the doors were locked. Convinced the area was quiet and the shop secure, she went back upstairs. She drew a hot bath and used some lavender oil she had found in the cabinet. The weariness seemed to melt away and she began making mental lists of things she needed to do. The first was to call her mother and then let the sheriff know she had moved.

Kit slid further down into the water and tried to figure out why she was confused by Tyler. He was the sheriff and should not be taking her concerns so lightly. Then again, he might be angry she was questioning his professional opinion. She had always admired him, especially the way he had cared for his handicapped brother, Mike.

She wondered why he never married. He was handsome, well-respected in the community and seemed a loving person. Her mind wandered to Tom and his demanding kisses. Tyler would be gentle, she mused and suddenly felt warm with the prospect of being held in Tyler's arms. She realized that it was the second time she had felt that way. "The sheriff?" she giggled embarrassed by the thought.

The phone's ringing jolted her to reality. She wrapped up in a towel and reached the bedroom extension by the fifth ring. She answered but no one spoke. Music was playing in the background, and it sounded like a loud restaurant or bar. "Hello, is anyone there?" she asked again. The other party hung up, and she was left holding the receiver with the dial tone sounding. She shivered, wondering if it was the same person who had sent her the notes. Or it could have been a drunk calling the wrong number.

Kit dressed in sweat pants and Bill's flannel shirt, and went to the kitchen to put some water to boil. Kit chose a blackberry blend and filled a metal tea ball with the loose tea.

She poured the hot water into the pot and dropped the tea ball inside to steep. She almost knocked the pot over when a tapping came at the back door. She hadn't heard anyone coming up the wooden stairs.

Kit was relieved when she saw Tyler Stone's smile. "Hello, Tyler," she said cheerfully, letting him into the kitchen area. "Join me for a 'spot of tea'?" she added with a British accent.

"Sure. Thought you'd like these," he said, producing a bouquet of flowers.

Kit was torn between enjoying their beauty and her immediate memory of the black orchid. Still questioning how often he used the florist she managed to say, "They're lovely. Thank you. I think there's a vase under the sink."

Tyler watched her as she rummaged under the sink, glad that she was looking away from him and didn't see his reaction to her bending over. "I called the Baker House earlier and they said you had already checked out."

She was right. She had seen a vase under the sink earlier that day, so she hauled it out, filled it half-way with water and put the flowers in it.

"I was going to let you know I'd moved in here as soon as I had my tea. I wasn't sure if Tom had told you." She put the vase on the table and stood back to admire them.

"No, he didn't. I would have helped, had I known," Tyler added apologetically.

Kit reached out and touched his arm. "That's kind, but, I know you're busy. Tom called the Waldens this morning and they helped."

Tyler's face reddened. He could have done that. He was angry with Tom for not saying anything and yet glad Kit understood how busy he was. However, Kit withdrew her hand, having read his reaction incorrectly. She put two cups and the sugar bowl on the table and motioned for him to sit down

"How did you get away from work?"

"Even the sheriff gets to have a lunch break."

"Sounds reasonable. Oh, I haven't anything to make for lunch."

"Already ate. Just wanted to see if you needed anything."

"Thanks. I think I'm set right now."

"How about a rain check?"

"I'd like that." She answered. Kit brought the tea pot to the table as well. "It's blackberry." She poured the tea for both of them and stirred some sugar into hers.

He sipped the hot brew. "No doubt one of Summer's teas," he smiled.

"Oh, so you know about Summer and Bill."

"Yes, we can talk about it some time." The phone rang and Kit jumped nervously. "Aren't you going to answer that?" Tyler asked.

"Yes. I was just wondering who would call here."

"It could be an old customer," he stated.

"Of course," she smiled and rose from the table. "Hello," she answered. "No, the book store is closed because of a death in the family. Yes, I'll watch for the book for you. You're very welcome. Goodbye."

Kit turned to Tyler. "You were right. It was a Mr. Guilder who is waiting for a book that Bill ordered for him. You know, it might take longer than I expected to close the shop. I hadn't thought of pending orders and so forth." She didn't sit down again but straightened up the counter.

Tyler sipped the tea. "You could put the store in an agent's hands. They would take care of all these details."

Kit didn't answer right away. She took the tea pot off the table and put it back on the counter. It gave her time to choose her words. She had not planned on bringing up her real motive for wanting to stay in Kensington, but the sheriff's apparent desire to have her leave spurred her on. She crossed her arms over her chest and leaned against the refrigerator door. "I need to stay, sheriff."

Tyler finished the tea and stood up. "Sheriff?" he chuckled. She really meant business, this tenacious young woman. The warm blue pools of her eyes had turned to ice once again and he was being shut out.

"Well, if you won't help me, Tyler, then I'll just have to think of you in an impersonal way. The man I used to know would care about what has been happening."

He walked over to her, laid his hands on top of her shoulders, and smiled. "Kathryn, I care deeply for your safety. I would very much like for you to stay right here in Kensington, but I'm concerned that you're chasing after a killer that just doesn't exist. Can you stay here without this vendetta?"

"I have a good job and friends back home. There's nothing here for me except memories. And I intend to be here until justice is served."

Tyler removed his hands. He realized Kit was not attracted to him in the least. "Be careful, little kitten." He smiled, kissed her softly on her forehead, and walked toward the door.

Kit shivered. His kiss had given her goose bumps! Before she could say anything, Tyler was letting himself out. He turned and said, "Make sure you lock this. Call if you need me," and he left, going down the steps as quietly as he had come up a short while ago. Only this time, he carried her lavender scent with him.

Kit locked the door and watched as the squad car pulled out of the alley. All of a sudden she felt very alone. Tom was at his sales meeting. She didn't know the neighbors, and someone, somewhere was sending her threatening notes. She could call Summer or even the Waldens but didn't want to appear irrational.

It was clear that Tyler, although caring, thought her ideas foolish and apparently wanted her to leave town. Suddenly, a frightening thought occurred to her. Perhaps this man she had respected as an old family friend and was clearly drawn to, had more to do with her brother's death than she wanted to believe.

THE PLAN – Chapter Two

Monday afternoon Kit changed into the capris she had brought with her and a patterned tank top. It was quite warm but she still wanted to go exploring in Kensington. Many things had changed in the year she was away. Stopping in and talking with Summer at the Mystic Spinner was her goal that day.

Kit lingered at the open door of the tobacco store. Although she did not smoke, the tobacco's aroma gave her a settled, earthy feeling. The owner saluted her with his Meerschaum pipe as he saw her.

The library was a popular place and she could tell that the small town enjoyed reading enough to support both the library and a book store.

There were several restaurants in town. "The Dive" was a tiny hole-in-the-wall restaurant. It was popular when Kit was in high school and it still attracted the high school set.

The Baker Hotel did a good morning business. An old-fashioned coffee shop catered mainly to area farmers and the Main Street business owners. Local and pro sports were openly debated there in the early hours as well as the sometimes conflicting weather reports. Then, there was Monique's, an upscale French Restaurant that many locals thought out of character for the town. Summer visitors and the village's ladies loved it for special occasions. There was an emergency care clinic, a satellite of the hospital 15 miles away. Overall, Kit knew Kensington to be a friendly, eclectic place to live.

The wind chimes tinkled merrily when she entered Summer's new age shop. The first thing she noticed was the shopkeeper dressed in a lightweight embroidered blouse with a calf-length butcher broom skirt and sandals.

"Greetings," Summer placed her hands together as if in prayer.

Kit, responding the same way smiled and answered, "Greetings to you." She wandered about the new age shop. It held unique and mystical gemstones and musical discs. The tarot cards and other devices for divining intrigued Kit, but did not hold her interest. The melodic wind chimes captured Kit's free spirit however, and she chose a wooden one.

Summer wrapped the chimes carefully. "The bamboo makes a natural wood-like sound. They can be very soothing."

She handed Summer her credit card. "I'm going to hang them on the back landing."

"They will like it there," Summer said. She handed the card back to Kit. "Please take these as a gift."

"Oh, I couldn't."

"You came to Kensington for a sad reason. Nevertheless, you have come back to your hometown. Their sound can bring you peace."

"Thank you," Kit answered but was too choked up to say anything more.

They skirted the subject of Bill, but both knew that one day they would address his death.

Walking back to the book store, Kit met one of her classmates pushing a stroller.

"Jennifer!" Kit reached out to hug her friend.

"Kathryn, I'm so glad to see you," Jennifer laughed as she hugged Kit.

"And who is this?" Kit asked bending down to look into the stroller.

"This is Trudy. She's almost one year old."

"Oh, Jennifer, she's adorable."

Trudy reached her pudgy hands to her mother as the corners of her little mouth went downward.

Kit stood up and smiled. "I think I scared her."

Jennifer laughed and handed Trudy a doll. "Here Sweetie." She smoothed Trudy's hair as she continued to talk with Kit.

"I felt so badly to hear about Bill. Are you doing okay?"

"As well as can be expected."

"Are you able to have a Coke or lemonade right now?"

"Yes."

"Perfect. Let's go to the Dive."

"Just like school, years ago," Kit laughed.

"Can you believe *ten* years ago?"

"It doesn't seem possible." They sat on one of the outside picnic tables.

"The town hasn't grown that much," Jennifer began. "There are a few new shops that cater to the tourists."

"I see that. Farms are still not very mechanized though."

"No. Daddy still has his truck farm but is now certified organic. Have you visited the Farmers' Market?"

"Not yet. That's something new since last year."

"Wednesdays and Saturday mornings in the library parking lot."

Kit giggled. "Sounds like you're a promoter."

"Actually, yes. Daddy found the organic market to be profitable instead of trendy. That's why he and other farmers still hire braceros from Mexico, along with local student labor. Have you seen the dark sedan parked near Monique's? It belongs to the labor boss for the braceros."

"I've seen the car. Its dark windows creep me out," Kit answered.

"Don't you know it! However, he keeps a tight rein on the workers. If they get in trouble he ships them back home."

"What kind of trouble?"

"Drinking, drugs, fighting mostly."

"In Kensington?"

"The sheriff has things under control. I think he has a good rapport with the boss in that regard."

"That's good to hear." Kit said. "It looks like the years have been good for you."

"Yes, somewhat. My husband and I both finished college. Chet did one tour in Iraq, survived intact – physically and mentally – and finished his service stateside. He worked for several years but has been unemployed for the last two."

"That must be difficult."

"Well, I actually got a job right after graduation and have been with the rehab office now for six years. It's worked out because I work and Chet takes care of Trudy."

"He must love it."

"We both like the arrangement. He's working on his Master's degree nights when I'm home with Trudy."

"Do you still do home care for handicapped patients?"

"Yes, it's rewarding to see people striving for independence."

"Do you remember Mike Stone?" Kit asked.

Jennifer met Kit's eyes. "Yes. I was his day time caregiver. His drowning made me sick at heart for weeks."

"Was he alone?"

"Yes, in a way. Tom had gone into the house to get something to eat for the men. When he returned to the pool area he found Mike drowned. Can we change the subject? Tell me about you."

"Well, I am an elementary school teacher."

"Like it?"

"Most of the time."

"Are you married or in a relationship?"

"Not now. I guess you didn't know that my husband died in an automobile accident."

"No, Kit. That must have been devastating."

"At times. I'm still dealing with it. This whole thing with Bill has made some heartaches surface."

Jennifer reached over and took Kit's hand. "Kit, we have to find ways to take our minds off the sadness."

"Any ideas?"

"There's always some way to help ourselves by helping others." Jennifer looked at her wrist watch. "And it's time for me to go home."

"Let's get together again," Kit smiled. She wondered if they actually would.

"We'll do that," Jennifer said as she and Kit parted company.

Sheriff Stone was pulling up outside of the book store when Kit returned.

"Looks like you've been shopping." He tipped his hat.

"Hello, Tyler. Yes and I had a delightful talk with Jennifer Lyons. Her little girl is already a year old."

"Nice family," Tyler answered. He removed his sun glasses.

Kit opened the front door and turned to Tyler. "So what brings you to my side of town?"

"You do."

"Should I be flattered?"

Tyler smiled broadly. "Depends."

"Upon what?" Getting information from Tyler was difficult.

"I'd like for us to spend some time together. I want to understand what you are thinking about Bill's death."

Kit visibly relaxed. "Thank you, Tyler. I'd like that also."

"Good. I'm on duty until 5 tonight. Would you like taking a walk?"

"I'll see you then." Kit's heart raced as Tyler left the store.

Tyler arrived a few minutes after 5 p.m. with a picnic basket..

"Hi there! I've just finished my book keeping chore for today," said Kit.

"Lots of paperwork?"

"Just mail orders. What's in the basket?"

"Supper."

"Why, Sheriff, when did you have time to do that?"

"I didn't. It pays to have a secretary," he grinned.

"So, where are we going?" Kit asked.

"Baker Park. It's not too far and it's cooler by the lake."

"Great. Give me a minute to lock up and I'll be ready."

Kit used the rest room, did a quick check of her hair, and came back into the book shop. Tyler was sitting on the window seat appearing lost in thought. Kit had the desire to put her arms around him and not go anywhere. Instead, she asked, "Ready?"

Tyler smiled and they left the shop, making sure the front door was locked. Summer was locking the front door to the Mystic Spinner and nodded to them as they walked by. Both Kit and Tyler waved to her.

"She's an incredible woman," Kit said.

"I agree. She and Bill were made for each other. We had such good times together." Tyler trailed off.

Kit slipped her arm through Tyler's. "You know, I just realized that you miss him too. I had just been thinking about myself and Summer. I'm sorry."

"You have more to worry about than me, Kitty. I'm glad you and Summer know each other."

"Yes, I think we could become friends."

"Looks like the park isn't too busy," Tyler said. "It's really quiet here in the mornings."

They chose a picnic table at the far end of the park as families were still playing in the water near the life guard's stand.

"Is this okay?" Tyler asked.

"It's fine." Kit smiled.

Tyler opened the basket and pulled out a table cloth. "Nothing fancy; got a jug of iced tea and some fried chicken. I'm starved after working all afternoon."

"This is more than I counted on; thought we were just taking a walk."

"Hope you don't mind."

"No, it really is okay," Kit answered.

"The president is taking the heat for not acting quicker in the gulf oil spill."

Kit tried to switch gears quickly. "And why did you think of that?"

"Oh, just looking at the ducks on the lake and thinking."

"It's awful for the birds on the gulf."

"Yep. Guess my mind is always working in several directions."

Kit boldly put her hand on Tyler's arm. "Do you ever relax?"

"Not often. Taking some time with you is about the limit."

Kit smiled. "I am flattered then, Sheriff."

Tyler covered her hand with his. "Just Tyler this evening, okay?"

Kit knew she wasn't going to be able to talk to him about her concerns of Bill's drowning. She decided to be bold however and be more personal. "Yes. I don't want to ruin an old friendship; but I am feeling very warm and peaceful when I'm with you."

Tyler leaned closer and kissed Kit's forehead. "Me too."

They finished their picnic and left when the mosquitoes started coming out. Kit hugged Tyler when they returned to the book store and he wanted to kiss her again, but did not. It was just too public.

"Goodnight, Sweetie. Make sure you lock up everything."

"I will, Ty. Thanks for the picnic." She went in. Tyler didn't leave until he saw her lock the door.

On Monday several customers had called the bookstore and Kit received a book delivery both Monday and Tuesday. On Tuesday evening Summer stopped in just before closing. "Greetings. I am going to the Farmers' Market early tomorrow. Would you like to go?"

"Yes, that would be great," Kit answered with genuine enthusiasm. "I usually go to the Lansing market each weekend."

"Ahh, but each market has its own personality. I think you'll enjoy this one."

"Time?"

"I'll be here at seven." Summer said.

" … a. m.?" Kit laughed.

Summer just smiled and nodded.

"Okay, I'll be ready," Kit answered.

Kit had to set the alarm to be sure to have time for coffee before meeting Summer. The sunlight was streaming through the window in the kitchen door by the time her new friend arrived on the back landing.

"Coffee?" Kit offered.

"No, thanks. Do you have a large bag like this?" Summer hooked her thumbs into the strap of a large cloth bag she had over her shoulder.

Kit thought a moment and took a shopping bag from her pantry. "This should do. Let's go then."

Summer checked on the hanging plants on the landing as Kit locked the door.

The library's parking lot was busy with people milling about and vendors setting up their booths.

"We're a tad early," Kit commented.

"We can watch the vendors' price 'wars'."

"Oh?"

"Yes. Notice their price signs are hand written. They check others' prices and adjust theirs accordingly. See how that man, his name is Ed, is writing something on his notepad?"

Kit nodded.

"He'll go back to his booth now and adjust his prices."

The women strolled by Jennifer's father Charlie's display, and noted the prices on the last of the strawberry crop; $5 a quart. The booth next to him held all varieties of annuals in hanging pots and mixed bouquets. From across the aisle the table filled with freshly-baked bread beckoned to Kit.

"I think your eyes just got bigger," Summer laughed.

"I will have to buy some of those cinnamon rolls, and at least one loaf of bread."

"The rolls sell quickly. I know."

They made their first purchase and tucked the baked treasures into their shopping bags.

A man displayed handmade jewelry in the next space. Kit admired the turquoise sets but she felt they were too expensive for her budget. A section of the table held fanciful earrings much like the ones Summer always wore. The tags attached read "Summer Breezes."

Kit looked up to see her friend talking to the vendor. When Summer turned around Kit announced, "These are yours."

"Yes. I sell them on commission," Summer stated and moved on leaving Kit to be impressed on her own.

"This free-range poultry farm doesn't use antibiotics or food additives. The eggs are delicious." Summer purchased a dozen brown-shelled eggs and carefully put them in her shoulder bag.

Kit made a mental note to buy a dozen the coming weekend. Another flower vendor followed that space. The next booth was a huge display of hydroponic fruits and vegetables. The following booth held honeys of all flavors.

Suddenly, Kit grabbed Summer's arm. "Look!" She nodded towards a young girl slipping apples into her oversized pants pockets. From out of nowhere an older teen put his arm about the girl's shoulder and steered her away from the booth.

"Happens all the time. The vendors are too busy at this time of the day to notice. We could go talk to the kids if you like."

"Someone has to."

The women followed the kids from a distance and held back when they saw them walking toward the dark sedan in the parking lot. The back seat window went down and the girl handed the apples to the person inside. She was given some cash and joyfully skipped away from the car. Soon, another bill was handed to the teen who shoved it into his jeans pocket.

"Just as Tyler thought," Summer shook her head.

"What?"

"Tyler has been thinking that the labor boss pays the braceros and their kids to do illegal things. If they are arrested, he bails them out and they get sent back to Mexico before it goes any further."

"No real proof?"

"Until now. We'll let him know," Summer said. "Come on, let's see if Ed's strawberries are less than Charlie's."

Ed's booth offered "last of the Michigan crop" of strawberries for $4.75 a quart.

Kit had arranged to meet her brother's lawyer, Henry James, at the shop that afternoon. He came in as Kit was dusting the bookshelves.

"I see you are smiling," Henry commented coming in.

"Yes. Look at the way the book genres are listed on the shelf sections. 'Previously Read Classics', 'Loved Favorites,' 'Adult Gems,' 'Read Aloud – Children,' and 'For a Cozy Fire'."

"Bill was never one to just say, 'Mystery' or 'Science Fiction'."

"That's for sure. Thank you for coming in, Henry."

"You are welcome. Here is a report of Bill's accounting."

Kit took a few minutes and looking over the report found that the shop was making a good profit. She began mulling over the idea of running the shop for the rest of the summer. It could veil her primary reason for being in Kensington. She wanted to search for the truth concerning her brother's death.

"I'll be available to help if you decide on selling," Henry said.

"Thank you. I'll let you know."

Kit filed the report in the office cabinet under the counter. She took out a calendar and crossed out the dates. She had only been in Kensington less than a week. In that time she buried her brother, inherited property, met a fascinating free-spirited woman, and fallen in love with the sheriff all over again. She had only begun to question Bill's death and had not really found out much. When was she ever going to have time to prepare lesson plans for the next school year?

Tyler called Kit on Thursday to see if she would have dinner with him Friday. She agreed if he would come to her place to eat.

He was at her back door Friday, with a bottle of wine, at 6 p.m. sharp.

Kit opened the door. "Hi. I thought you'd be in uniform."

"Hello," He hugged her with one arm and then handed her a St. Julian's wine. "I took off early."

She led the way into the kitchen. "Glad you did. Thanks for the wine." She moved across the kitchen and rummaged around in the drawer for the bottle opener.

Tyler opened the bottle while Kit took the lasagna out of the oven to cool. She took two glasses from the cupboard. "Would you like to sit on the landing?"

"Sure, it's cooler now." He led the way to the landing and sat on the glider.

Kit joined him and watched his jaw muscles flexing as he poured. "Have you found anything new in your investigation of Bill's death?"

Tyler drank half of the glass of wine and then shook his head. "Kit, there aren't enough of us on the force to do much more than the initial investigation. There have been several incidents with the migrant teens."

"I was afraid of that. So, there really is a problem here?"

"I've pretty much figured out how the kids are being controlled. They like the thrill of doing what their boss wants because they know if they're caught their only punishment will be they are sent back to Mexico – to their friends and families."

"What type of things are they doing?"

"Mischief mostly. Some graffiti, some prank calls."

"Do you think the notes and calls I'm getting could be them?"

Tyler drained his glass. "It could be, Kit. I haven't been able to make the connection though."

"Connection?"

"Yep. If it's at the bidding of the migrant boss, there would have to be some connection between you and his group."

"Mob, you mean?"

"Technically, yes."

"The Mexican mob killed my brother?"

"That's not what I'm saying. It doesn't make sense."

"No, it doesn't."

"Can we eat now? I'm starved."

"Sure." She placed her hand on his arm. "Thanks for looking into it."

Tyler caressed her cheek with his fingertips. "You know I'll help you if I can."

Kit leaned forward to kiss his cheek and Tyler pulled her closer to him. He kissed her lightly until she responded. They both allowed their passion to carry them into a deep embrace. The couple sat molded to one another for a long while. Neither spoke. Neither wanted to break apart. It wasn't until Tyler's stomach gave out a large growl that the two of them laughed, got up and went inside to eat.

It rained Saturday and there weren't as many people on the streets. Summer came into the book store about 10 a.m. She had a large colorful scarf about her head and shoulders. "Greetings!" she called out gaily.

"What brings you out in the rain?" Kit laughed as Summer shook the rain from her scarf.

"I started thinking about the Fourth and the sidewalk sales we all participate in. Suddenly it dawned on me that you might not have known about it."

"Oh, in the past, when I've been in Kensington on the Fourth, I shopped at the sales. I just didn't think about how this year I could participate."

"Well, it is two weeks from now, but it never is too early to start planning."

"Thanks. I've got some extra stock I could put on sale; maybe even a have a raffle."

"That's the spirit."

"Tyler probably has to work. Would you like to pal around after the parade? Better yet, even if Tyler has to work, we could all go together."

"If you're sure I won't be a third wheel."

"Of course not. It could be fun," Kit said.

Kit did make an effort to attend church on Sunday. She was greeted warmly. Elly and Gus Walden were especially glad to see her there. They introduced her to almost everyone after the service. She smiled and made small talk and was glad to finally get outside in the fresh air where the minister and his wife waited to shake hands with the congregation.

The minister asked how long she would be staying, and Kit answered, "I'm going to be here until the last week of August." There, she thought. That settled that question.

Elly nodded her head. "I'm so glad to hear that, dear." Other churchgoers nearby echoed her sentiment, and Kit was beginning to feel more at home.

Kit walked across the town square toward the bookstore and recognized Tom's silver Porsche parked in front. She waved to the figure leaning against the car. As she approached, his smile broadened, but the mirror-finished sunglasses hid his eyes. "Feel like a picnic?"

"Sure. Give me a few minutes to change!" Kit responded and opened the shop's front door. "Make yourself comfortable. I'll be right out," she added and went upstairs to the living quarters. What was it about the Stone men and picnics?

She hurriedly threw on a pair of jeans, a tank top and her tennis shoes. She grabbed one of the cable knit sweaters she had saved from her brother's wardrobe and draped it over her back, tying the arms about her neck. She drew her hair away from her face, securing it with a colorful neck scarf. She looked in the mirror and giggled. Maybe some of her mother's haphazard fashion was born out of haste.

Tom was leafing through some pamphlets on new books. "All set?" he asked.

"All set," she answered and then added, "Is there anything I should bring along?"

Nope, just your appetite. I got a basket from Monique's Restaurant."

"A French picnic? Trés bon!" she smiled and held the door open for him. She locked the shop once again and turned to see Tom watching her.

He started the engine and slipped his sunglasses on again. Those darn glasses, she thought as she slid into the car's bucket seat. Being unable to see his eyes made her uneasy. It reminded her of the state trooper who had stopped her for speeding last year. He too had been wearing mirrored sunglasses. It gave her the feeling of impending doom. She suddenly felt chilled and drew the sweater about her closer.

Tom had not spoken but was out of town quickly, shifting gears flawlessly. He glanced her way expressionless and turned down the air conditioning.

Kit was going to thank him but she could tell by his jaw muscles flexing that he was lost in his own thoughts.

Instead she said, "You're back in town earlier than I expected."

"Yes. The business didn't take as long as I expected."

Within a few minutes they turned onto the road that wound around to the North side of the lake. She caught her breath and felt her heart pounding. She and her brother had always fished the South and West parts of the lake with their father.

Tom said, "I know a nice spot on the North side. It's sunny this time of day."

Kit nodded but stared straight ahead. At least it wouldn't be where they found Bill's body.

Tom parked just off the roadway. "Be careful. This spot is ideal for a private picnic."

Kit was glad for her wearing her "tennies." They climbed down a narrow path through the trees to reach the secluded cove. The sunlight cast a warm glow on the beach. The sand was dotted by spots of shade from the overhanging willow branches. The light glistened on tiny ripples and Kit quietly followed the shore line across the water.

"Thought you'd like it," said Tom. "Things haven't changed much on the lake."

Kit had such great memories of the lake, but now the thought that her brother's life ended there clouded her feelings. "What's the board fence over there? asked Kit, trying to put her thoughts on hold.

Tom grinned. "Sun Harbor, or Sin Harbor as some local folk call it."

"What?" Kit smiled, amused at Tom's statement.

"Local nudist park." Tom held the blanket up and Kit helped him spread it on the sand.

"How long has it been here?"

"Last couple of years. Didn't you know?"

"No," giggled Kit. "Looks like enlightenment has arrived in Kensington!"

Tom shook his head in amazement. "You can't mean that."

"Of course I can. Kensington has been so outdated."

"There's a thing about decency."

"Education, tolerance, freedom are better words," Kit said.

"Okay." Tom did not want to argue, especially today. "Let's eat. I'm starved." He stretched out on the blanket leaving Kit to explore the basket.

It contained a wondrous meal of turkey sandwiches, melon, cut veggies and a bottle of rosé Chablis and plastic glasses. Tom had a cork screw packed and deftly used it to uncork the Chablis. He poured each of them a glass. "You will see this compliments the broasted turkey," he began but Kit rolled her eyes and laughed.

Kit sat cross-legged on the blanket handing him a sandwich. "How long have you been a wine aficionado?"

"It must be the travels. 'Here's a lovely Madeira, my dear,'" he said with a husky whisper.

"I know the joke, Tom," Kit gave him a smirk to dismiss his reference to an off-color poem about seduction. "Here," have some of this lovely meal."

Tom ate his sandwich in silence. He had a second glass of wine with a dish of melon. "The lake is beckoning. Wouldn't you like to go swimming?"

Kit ignored him and bit her lip slightly. "Do you remember how the crowd we ran around with would come here at night and have a camp fire?"

"And sing dumb songs – and drink beer – and make out," Tom answered.

"That was eons ago."

"We all know a lot more now about life – and fine wines – and making love instead of making out." Tom gave her that condescending smile again.

"You sure are full of yourself," she thought, but said, "Age doesn't always make us wiser though."

"And what is it that you want to know?"

"What I really want to know is if you have turned up any clues. Did you have a busy schedule this past few weeks?" Kit asked.

Tom's mood shifted. "Yes. The company has expanded its territory. I didn't have time to get back to you, but I did talk with the florist."

"Great!" she said, impatient for the report.

Tom swirled the Chablis about in the wine glass. How he loved to dramatize things, thought Kit. She found herself blurting out, "Well?"

Tom finally removed his sunglasses and smiled at her. "A tad impatient, Kitty?" Kit playfully hit him on the shoulder with the red and white checkered napkin. "Okay, okay." He laughed. "Actually, there's nothing that will help us. The florist didn't know a thing. The black orchid could have come from anywhere," he stated and drained his wine.

Kit frowned. "Well, strike one."

"But the ball game isn't over," he grinned, took her wine glass from her and pulled her closer, making her lose her balance. Before she could recover, he moved her about so that she was stretched out on her back beside him, his arm under her head. She was going to protest, but he was talking about the cloud formations overhead.

Kit relaxed and listened. "What do you see over that way?" Tom asked as he pointed to the East.

"It looks like a bunny," she laughed.

Tom clucked his tongue and said, "No, it's a triceratops! What about over that way?" he asked, his arm sweeping across her toward the other horizon. He brought his head closer to hers to help her find the line of vision.

Kit tried to remain calm, but she knew he was maneuvering. "It looks like a hummingbird."

Tom looked deeply into her eyes, just inches away from her face. "If you look closer I'll bet you can see a hawk, its talons swooping down to intercept your bunny!"

Kit started laughing. "I thought you said it was a triceratops. Your hawk just became a cooked goose!"

That brought a laugh from Tom, and he lay back looking skyward again. Suddenly he sat up and kicked off his shoes. "Let's go swimming!"

"I didn't bring a suit!" Kit stammered.

"Well, we could go over to Sun Harbor and you wouldn't need one." Tom grinned lasciviously and wiggled his eyebrows at her.

Kit had intended to comment about social nudity when Tom caught her off guard by rolling toward her, pulling her closer. He gathered both of her hands over her head and pinned her down with one hand and massaged the small of her back with the other. "I guess we'll just have to find another way to entertain ourselves."

"Tom ..." she began but her words were cut short as he crushed his mouth to hers. She tried to free herself without being overly forceful but his strength was overpowering. Suddenly he froze and jerked his head up. It was then that Kit heard the whine of a powerboat's motor. Tom cursed under his breath and sat up. Kit, relieved the struggle was over, sat up and watched the sheriff's patrol boat approaching.

"I wouldn't be surprised if it were big brother," Tom growled and glared toward the water.

A deputy waved and Kit waved back. The muscles in Tom's jaws relaxed as the boat cruised by. He grabbed his shoes and shoved his feet into them. Tom was once fun-loving. Kit now saw him taking on a more demanding attitude; and when he didn't get what he wanted, he reverted to being a spoiled child.

Kit began picking up the picnic items and repacked the basket. "You seem to have some animosity toward your brother. When did that begin?"

"Shows, huh?" Tom said flatly. "Well, it would be just like him to come check up on me. You know he's power crazy."

Kit watched as Tom shook out the blanket. At least the elder Stone was a gentleman. She wondered why Tyler would be checking up on his brother. "Would he be crazy enough to hurt someone?" Kit asked suddenly.

Tom looked at her for a moment and answered quietly, "Maybe." He grabbed the basket and led the way back to his car.

Kit had to scramble to keep up with him. Why did everything seem to point to the possibility that Tyler Stone was a dangerous man?

On the ride back to town, Kit told Tom about the book orders she had been able to fill and her intention to stay until she had to go back to her teaching job. Sighing heavily he slowed the vehicle and said, "I'll be glad when you're safe at home with Amanda. I'm not thoroughly convinced your brother was murdered."

"If there is any chance I can find some evidence; I want to be here to see that justice is done."

"You can be sure the good people of Kensington will see to that," Tom said sarcastically.

Kit noted his attitude and said, "I've been relying on you and the sheriff and need to really start investigating myself."

"That can be dangerous, Kitty. You can't rely on anyone else here to help."

Kit asked, "You're not very happy living here, are you?"

"Not really. I feel trapped, but big brother needs me," Tom sighed again.

"I see," Kit answered. But she did not understand. The Tyler family must have some skeletons hidden away. Heaven knows that her family closet had a few.

"What's the next step in our investigation?" she asked.

"I'll be in town for a few days and will talk with some local fishermen. I'll be in touch. Here we are, safe and sound," he grinned as they pulled up outside the store.

Kit hesitated but reached for the door when he made no effort to help her. She climbed out and said, "Thanks, Tom. I'll wait to hear from you."

He gave her a two-fingered salute and she shut the door. What an odd afternoon, she thought as he sped away.

She let herself into the book shop and looked about. She walked from shelf to shelf, admiring the neat order. The section on previously-read classics was her favorite. Her brother never called them "used" books. Indeed, some of the volumes were bound with tooled leather and a few were signed copies. Perhaps her brother was killed over the possession of a rare book. The only way she could find out was to learn more about the books – and to formally re-open the store. She would be there for the rest of the summer anyway.

Kit searched under the counter and finding white poster board and colored felt markers, skillfully penned a "Re-Opened for Business" sign. It would be put in the window in the morning. A working business might sell more readily.

The phone rang and Kit, sure it was her mother, answered, "Hello, Mom!" but no one responded. "Hello, this is Bates' Books," she answered again.

The receiver was hung up on the other end and Kit was not sure whether to be angry or frightened. She chose the anger and began cleaning with a fury. After a half-hour, she decided to tackle the file cabinet in the office that she had been ignoring since she moved in.

The first drawer contained the past four years' tax returns and records of dealers and their various catalogs. The second drawer held her brother's keepsakes plus things of her father's – pictures of Kit, a scrapbook filled with her letters, copies of term papers and other memorabilia from his life.

She found Bill's high school year book and sat down to read the autographs on the front pages. She laughed when she saw her eight-year-old handwriting telling her brother "to not get into trouble." She flipped to the senior section to see his picture. He was a real looker, she thought, but what a haircut! A few pages later Tyler Stone's picture smiled up at her. He was so thin then, he actually improved with age. Even then he had the air of being a leader. She noted he was the captain of the basketball team and participated in many other extra-curricular activities as well. She turned to the sports section and read about the championship basketball team. Mike Stone, Tyler's younger brother, was star athlete quality and had won several awards. She remembered with dismay how Mike had been hurt in that terrible car accident after the championship.

Kit flipped through the rest of the book absently, wondering about the accident when she noticed the back pages held some newspaper clippings.

It was getting late, so Kit locked up the shop, turned off the lights, and climbed the dimly lit stairs to the living quarters. She took the year book into the kitchen, brewed some tea, and settled at the table to read.

The first clipping told about the Raiders team and the strong junior center, Mike Stone. A few more clippings showed the team cutting down the net after winning the state championship. The next item was an account of a car accident that killed one of the basketball team's members, Jim Banks, and injured four others, Matt Spencer, Bill Bates, David Melton, and Mike Stone. A follow-up article revealed that injuries from the accident had permanently disabled the Raider's star, Mike Stone. The article also reported that other team members, including Don Greyson, Tyler Stone, Pete Jackson, Dan Gregory and Burt White were not injured.

    The story explained that the boys had been at the lake celebrating their championship and had been drinking. The driver was given probation. The townspeople felt the boys had suffered enough and jointly pleaded leniency for the driver. Was that the basis for Tom's statement about the townspeople seeing that justice was done?

    Kit's mind reeled. Her brother had limped slightly since the accident but never discussed it with her as she was so much younger than he. She knew that the accident had been the cause. Her brother had also included clippings about other team members and Kit read of the death of one of the boys, Sid Tysen, in "Desert Storm."

    He had kept a death notice for Matthew Spencer. She read how in July of 2008, his car careened off the Old River Road bridge; and he was drowned. The police investigation showed that another vehicle might have been involved, but nothing was ever discovered. It was noted that Spencer had been the driver of the car the night that Jim Banks had been killed, back in 1990.

    Another clipping, dated September 2008, two months after Spencer's death, told of Michael Stone's accidental drowning in the pool of his brother, Sheriff Tyler Stone, with whom he resided. Kit took a deep breath and turned the article face down on the table. A small red "12" was scrawled on the back. She picked up Spencer's obituary and hastily turned it over. A number "10" was there. Tysen's obituary had an "8" on the back. What was her brother trying to say?

    Kit read the back of the most recent clipping. Yes, there was a red "6" on the back. It was the death notice of David Melton. About one year ago Melton had been electrocuted. The space heater he was using had slipped off the chair next to the tub, where he was bathing, and into the water. Stupidity or intention? Kit wondered. This would be a good place to start to look for clues.

Her brother's drowning was just too much of a coincidence. She turned back to the picture of the basketball team. The red numbers coincided with the jersey numbers. Bill Bates had kept track of his team members' deaths. Four more men were represented in the picture - three of whom she did not recognize. The fourth was Tyler Stone. Perhaps he was in danger instead of being responsible.

Kit went to the phone, intending to call Tyler about the discovery, but what did it prove anyway? Maybe Tom was right and Tyler was a little crazy. Maybe the accident had left him slightly unbalanced.

The thought of Tyler Stone being a murderer went against everything Kit believed about the man. After all the years of Tyler having an honorable reputation, she owed him the benefit of the doubt.

Kit remembered the summer after her graduation and the horrendous crush she had on the then "deputy" Stone. Somehow, she always thought if she had just been a few years older he would have responded to all of her tactics. When their eyes met, there had been such promise, but Tommie was always around; and she didn't have a chance to be alone with Tyler. Even so, there had been a magnetism between them – one that still seemed alive, especially with their spending time together.

Kit took a deep breath and went back downstairs into her brother's office. She dug out the newspaper that contained the notice of his death. With trembling hands she clipped the notice out and found a red pencil.

She took them back to the kitchen and looked at the team picture once again. She wrote "14," the number on her brother's jersey, on the back of the clipping and put it with the others. She took the year book into her bedroom and put it on the dresser.

Kit called her mother and discussed her plans to re-open the bookstore.

"I always knew books were in your bloodstream, Sweetie. You're a good choice to take over Bill's business," Amanda said supportively.

"It won't be permanent, Mom, but perhaps it will pay expenses while I'm here," Kit answered.

"You're planning to come back here to teach this fall?"

"Of course. I should find a buyer by then."

"You're not bothering Tyler about Bill's death, are you?"

"No, Mom. I don't see him that often."

"Pity. Well, take care of yourself. 'Love you!" she added cheerfully.

"Love you, too!" Kit answered and hung up the receiver. That was an odd remark about it being a pity she was not seeing Tyler often.

Kit ate a light supper and then read for a while. Throughout the night she tossed and turned, alternately sleeping and waking. She tried to come up with theories to tie the team members' deaths together and there always was a hole in the theory. She decided she would find out about the other three team members and that meant speaking with Tyler Stone.

In the morning Kit put the "open" sign in the window and called the newspaper. She asked them to run an item about the re-opening of the store and they said they would do so. She then called the sheriff's office and left word for Tyler to call her at his convenience. Less than fifteen minutes later he arrived at the store.

"What's this?" He greeted her smiling, and pointed to the sign.

"Good morning, Tyler! I'm glad you stopped in. Did you get my message?"

"Yes. That's why I'm here."

"Fine. I wanted you to know I've re-opened the store.

I figured as long as phone orders were doing so well, I'd try the general public as well."

"Are you still looking for a buyer?"

"By all means." The phone rang and Tyler went to the window display. Kit answered some questions on large print books that were on the shelf, and then she walked to where Tyler was inspecting a poetry book.

"I guess I'd better change the display. New arrivals are coming in every day. I was wondering if you could meet me for lunch today."

"Sorry, Kathryn, I stopped in on my way to a seminar at the Capital, but I'll be back Wednesday afternoon. How about Wednesday for supper?"

Kit said, "That will work. Where should I meet you?"

Tyler smiled. "I'd rather pick you up if you don't mind. Safer that way. Leave a message for me at the office if there's a problem, otherwise I'll pick you up at 7:30."

"It's a date," Kit smiled.

Tyler smiled and then handed her the book he had been looking at. "I'll take this."

"Seriously?" she asked.

He pulled out his wallet and offered her the money and she rang up the amount on the old cash register. She began to put it in a bag and he stopped her. "Not needed," he said and took his pen from his pocket and scribbled something in the front.

"I've enjoyed this immensely. This is for you." Kit was astonished. Her first non-phone customer was giving the book back to her.

"Tyler?" she questioned. She certainly had many things to learn about him.

"It's yours," he reassured her. "See you Wednesday at 7:30."

She nodded and then added, "Drive safely."

He smiled and left. His spicy aftershave lingered on the air for a while; and once again she prayed he had nothing to do with the murders.

Murders? Well, the other deaths could have been arranged too!

Kit opened the poetry book to where Tyler had penned, "It is the best gift, T. S."

She looked at the title again, *The Gift of Love*, and began reading a few of the pages. She discovered they were all love sonnets, songs of love and light verse of the same topic. Off and on during the morning, she read from the book and began to realize Tyler Stone was a romantic if he enjoyed this book. She imagined him relaxing before the fireplace, reading and smoking his pipe with that special cherry blend tobacco. Did he still use his pipe? Was he trying to tell her something?

Her daydreaming was interrupted by the tinkle of the bell on the door. It was Summer Moon.

Summer had on a cool blue caftan with a handkerchief hem and long sweeping sleeves. As usual, her jewelry jingled and sparkled in the light.

"Good Morning!" Kit greeted her warmly,

"Greetings, Kathryn," she began hesitantly. "It's been difficult, and I was hurting so bad this morning that I just had to be near." Summer's composure began to crumble.

Kit took Summer's hand in hers in a gesture of comfort. After a moment, Summer withdrew her hand and looked for a tissue in her purse. "Come sit with me," Kit offered and walked toward the window seat at the back of the shop. "Had you been seeing Bill for a long time?"

Summer followed Kit and sat next to her. "I moved to Kensington about a year ago. I like to read, so the discovery of this shop was wonderful. After a few weeks, Bill and I discussed the books we were reading and that led to lunches and eventually to our falling in love. I feel so cheated."

"I'm sorry, Summer. Obviously we both have lost someone we loved."

Summer didn't speak but just nodded her head. Soon she looked at Kit. "Please call me "Sam" – everyone else does."

"Sam?" Kit asked surprised. Her brother's letters were filled with all the interesting things he and his best buddy, 'Sam' were up to. "Did you go fishing and rock hunting with Bill?"

"Why, yes. How did you know?"

"From letters, but I thought you were his friend – a man."

"Friend, yes – man, no!" she smiled.

"Let me get something for you. I'm sure Bill would want for you to have it." Kit went to the back porch and returned a moment later with a denim captain's hat. Several fancy fishing lures were hooked into the material. She handed it to Summer.

Summer's face paled. "Bill never went fishing without his lucky hat."

Kit understood immediately. "Bill supposedly drowned while fishing." Summer stared at the hat and Kit continued. "Do you think it was an accident?"

Summer said quietly, "I've had my suspicions all along. His tackle box and rod were in the boat. The boat was found adrift along the western shore."

"Yes, that's where we usually fished," nodded Kit.

"But his body was found along the Southern edge. The coroner theorized he had fallen overboard in the middle of the lake and tried to swim for the closest shore. They said his heart gave out and he drowned."

"I don't believe that for a minute."

"Neither do I, Kathryn."

Kit realized she had another ally. "There's so much going on with re-opening the store. I advertised for a buyer. Some day I'm going to tackle lesson plan ideas for the fall. But what I really want to do is to look for answers. I'm going to prove Bill didn't drown accidentally. Bill's hat being here is a sign." Kit said solemnly.

The women stared at Bill Bates' fishing hat and Summer answered, "I'll do all I can to help."

The phone rang and Kit answered, "Bates Books."

"Go home," was the growled reply.

"Who is this?" Kit demanded, but the line went dead.

"Kathryn, what's wrong?"

"I've been getting warnings to leave town – like that."

"Have you told Sheriff Stone?

"Yes. He's going out of town for a couple of nights, but we have an appointment Wednesday." She evaded any further discussion about him and added, "Do you have time for lunch so we can compare notes?"

"That would be fine. I spent a great deal of my time here before," and her voice trailed off. She took a deep breath. "I'd be glad to help you order, restock shelves and so forth."

Kit had seen the paycheck stubs written out merely to "Sam" and it suddenly dawned on her that her brother's lady friend was also a part time employee. "Well, I suppose I could pay you."

"No, that's totally unnecessary. Bill insisted, so I took the money. I'm glad you reminded me." She dug into her purse again and brought out a check. "I put it all into a savings account. I'm independently wealthy – what can I say?" she grinned. "Bill and I were planning to marry and this extra money would have been an added nest egg. I want you to have it, Kathryn."

Kit took the check. "This means we can hire an investigator if we need to."

"Just be careful. I don't like the idea of the murderer knowing you are looking for him."

Kit nodded. Impulsively she hugged Summer. She liked this casual, down to earth woman who smelled of patchouli and had an instant smile.

"I'll go to Monique's early to get us a table if you like," Summer offered.

"That sounds great," Kit nodded, "I'll see you at noon."

Summer paused at the door before leaving and gave Kit a solemn look, nodded and was gone.

Suddenly Kit thought Bill's last will and testament was probably going to be changed to include Summer. The killer took more than one life that day.

Kit was optimistic about meeting with Summer in spite of had happened and was glad the morning flew by. The idea of offering "Sam" a partnership in the bookstore had come to her as she walked to the little French restaurant.

"Monique's" was run by Monica Lasky, a young woman that Kit had known while in junior high school. She was as un-French as anyone in the town, but possessed just the right qualities to take a unique idea and make a go of it.

"Katríne, my old friend," Monica purred in a French accent as Kit entered the dimly lit foyer.

Kit smiled, surprised that Monica was the hostess.

"Hello, Monica, it's been a long time."

"It is 'Monique', mon cher, and ouí, it has been far, far too long. I am so pleased you have come to my establishment. Come, come, Summer is waiting for you."

Monica ushered Kit past the dining room, through lovely walnut doors and back into the bright sunshine. The patio held several white wrought iron tables with blue and white umbrellas and Summer held up her drink to salute Kit's arrival.

"I do so love the luncheon set," Monica gushed in the same French accent. "That is why I make it a point to be here to greet my customers." She handed Kit a menu and snapped her fingers. Pete Larson, the waiter, appeared as quickly as Monica left.

"She'll have the same, Pierre," Summer motioned the waiter away with her drink and turned her attention to Kit. "You look amused, mon cher," she smiled.

"I guess you could say that," Kit giggled and the two women could hardly keep their laughter under control.

"Pierre" returned with a tall glass of sparkling water

with a twist of lemon for Kit. "I'll have the Caesar salad," Summer said.

Kit ordered a fresh fruit platter and sipped the iced water and watched Summer watch her.

"You are very much like him, you know."

"Both Bill and I resembled Dad more than Mother," Kit agreed. "I think I inherited the best qualities from both of them." She grinned and that brought more peals of laughter from both women.

"You have the same sense of humor, as well; and that is the last I am going to compare you to Bill. I want to know you for you, Kathryn."

"Please call me 'Kit'. I would like to know more about you as well."

"Ah, yes, the mystic spinner of tales. You do not seem intimidated by my persona."

"You dress so very much like my mother – only more, shall I say 'bohemian.' That shows a love for spontaneity and appreciation for color and movement."

"Most of the townspeople ignore me now. At first, they thought I was a wicked witch. Most of my customers are from the cities nearby."

"A wicked witch, eh?" Kit giggled.

"Oh, I am different, but I am not, I assure you, wicked. I don't want all that evil sent back to me!"

"You certainly are a free spirit, and I can see how Bill was attracted to you!"

"And I didn't even cast a spell on him." Summer said. She didn't even try to hide a smile. However, as quickly as she smiled, her loss descended on her again and she looked away and took a deep breath.

"I am from California originally. My husband of 15 years was a farmer." She sipped her water. Kit nodded, listening. "He grew grapes in the Napa Valley, as did his father and grand father and great grand father before him. When he died, I was given a grand sum of money that he set aside for me. I moved here to Michigan to repair my spirit. And Bill was responsible for a great deal of that healing."

Tears fell from Kit's eyes unchecked. "I'm so glad you and he were happy. I never thought he'd find anyone. I was married for less than two years, and it doesn't seem right that Gregg was taken away so soon either."

"All things are as they need to be in the universe, my friend."

Kit touched Summer's hand. "I hope we are going to be good friends. I also have an idea I hope you will consider. I am going to be going back home after the end of August, and the book store will need an owner. Would you consider at least part ownership for the time being so that the business won't fall apart?"

"Well, if you let me consider the idea for a while," Summer said thoughtfully. She sipped her water and then smiled, "Yes, I like the idea."

Kit offered Summer her hand and she grasped it firmly. "Partners!"

"Partners!"

"We already are partners in trying to solve Bill's ..."

"... ah, our lunch has arrived," Summer interrupted Kit. After Pierre left Summer whispered, "This is a small town with large ears, 'mon cher'. We must make it a point to be careful what is said."

Kit nodded, the joviality gone for the moment. "I probably am too trusting at times," she said quietly.

"So, enjoy your fruit. I doubt it is poisoned."

Kit was shocked at the thought but then read the humor in Summer's eyes. She could tell it would be an interesting friendship.

While walking back toward their respective shops Summer announced, "I'd really like to introduce you to some fine friends of mine and Bill's."

Kit smiled broadly. "I'm touched that you would want to."

"It may take a stretch in your spiritual growth,

however," Summer said softly as they arrived at her shop. She motioned to the bench by the door. Kit loved the mystery and sat down, wondering what her friend meant.

Summer sat close by and spoke quietly. "Bill and I are, were rather," she reminded herself aloud, "naturists. I still am, but I'd like you to experience the lifestyle."

Kit interrupted her smiling, "Naturists – not naturalists – nudists you mean?"

Summer, not changing her expression, nodded her head "yes."

"Oh my goodness," Kit paled. "Sin Harbor!"

It was Summer's turn to giggle. "So you've heard. Truly, Kit, social nudism is a wonderful experience. I think you could relax."

"Well, I don't think I need to get naked to find myself."

"I didn't say that, Kit. I thought perhaps you'd like to meet some of Bill's friends. Besides, we shouldn't leave any stones unturned," Summer said slyly but Kit missed the meaning.

"Get to the naked truth, eh?" Kit responded and both women broke into laughter.

"I'm going to camp there tomorrow night. You're welcome to come along. Things have been rather chaotic for you and it would help to put some distance between you and your heckler." Summer offered.

Kit stood up. "Thanks, Summer. I'll think about it. Would you like to help in the store tomorrow morning?"

"Sure, I'd really like that. What are you up to today?" asked Summer.

"I'm not having much business, so I'm going to use the library microfiche and look up some newspaper records on David Melton."

"He died about a year ago, didn't he?"

"Yes," Kit answered. It looks suspicious to me.

"Kit, he died at home."

"Yes."

"Good luck then. I'm going back to my shop."
"Thanks, I'll let you know if I find anything."

    Kit closed the book store at three and went to the library. She took David Melton's death notice that her brother had kept. In minutes she was reading the microfiche machine article. Her one semester of doing library research years was paying off by understanding how to use the machine and the benefits of reading actual articles.

    Kit flipped through the index until she found the headline "David R. Melton, Local Resident Found Dead in His Home, February 15, 2009." The article went on to say that David, a widower, lived alone. He was taking a bath and apparently using a space heater too near the bathtub. The heater fell into the tub and electrocuted him. He was found by a local teenager who was at Melton's home, shoveling snow. Survivors include his son, Alan from Pittsford.

    A teenager had been sitting nearby. Kit was sure she was watching her, so when she was done with the research Kit turned and smiled at her. It gave the girl an open door. "I've always wondered how that works," she said to Kit in a Mexican accent.

    "It's not difficult. I'm sure the librarian can show you how."

    The girl came out of her seat and was at Kit's elbow, looking at the screen. "It still looks difficult to me."

    Kit had the feeling she was trying to read the information so she quickly pressed the button to print the article. The screen went black and the girl moved away without saying anything else.

    It only took her a few minutes to walk back to the book store. Allan Melton's phone number was listed, so she called from the store office.

    "Hello," Melton answered.

    "Hello. This is Kathryn Anderson. I'm Bill Bates' sister.

"Oh, Mrs. Anderson, I was sorry to read about Bill's death."

"Thank you. I was wondering if I could ask you some personal questions, being that your father and my brother were friends."

"You may ask."

"Thank you. I wanted to know about the teenager that found your father."

"That was a freak situation. I didn't even know that Dad was hiring anyone to shovel his walk. The kid said he had finished the walk and wanted to get paid. He knocked several times and went in because Dad didn't answer. He heard a noise in the other room and saw a flash."

"Didn't he call anyone?"

"Yes, but not until he investigated himself. He found Dad in the tub and then called the police."

"Did you talk to the young man?" Kit asked.

"No. After arrangements for Dad were made I tried. But, his family said the teen was so shaken, he went back to Mexico to live with his grand parents."

"Did you think anything different about his death?"

"Well, at the time the coroner said that Dad probably slipped in the tub and drowned."

"Did he hit his head?"

"Yes. He tried to get up and doing so knocked the heater into the water."

"I'm so sorry."

"It was rather strange. Why do you want to know?"

"Bill was an excellent swimmer and the coroner said his death was from drowning. Also, he had a bruise on his forehead."

"I don't think the coincidences are related," Melton said.

"More than likely not. But, I appreciate your indulging my curiosity."

"You're welcome. Again, my condolences."

Kit hung up the phone and called Summer immediately. "Are you busy?"

"Not too busy for you. What did you learn?"

"I think Melton was killed. Hit over the head and drown and the space heater thrown into the tub to make it look like an accident. Alan Melton told me a teenager found him but Alan never had a chance to talk to him. He went back to Mexico to live."

"Sounds too convenient."

"Yes; there's another thing," Kit answered.

"What?"

"A Mexican girl was very forward at the library today in trying to see what I was doing."

That night, Kit spoke with Amanda about the progress made with the book store. She deliberately left out any information about her ongoing investigation. "I met the auburn haired woman from the funeral, Mom."

"Oh, really? Who is she?"

"Summer Moon, the proprietress of The Mystic Spinner new age shop."

"I drooled over some of the jewelry I saw in the window while I was there. How did you meet her?"

"Well, I went into the shop and the rest is history. She was in love with Bill."

Amanda didn't answer, so Kit continued, "And they were talking about marriage, Mom."

Amanda cleared her throat and sniffled. Her voice cracked as she said quietly, "I'm so thankful that Bill had someone to love."

"I've offered her a partnership in the book store."

"That sounds like a good idea," Amanda stated, and Kit knew she was not crying any longer.

"It is a good idea," Kit responded.

"And how are the Stone brothers?"

"Impossible to understand," Kit chuckled.

"Well, behave yourself, youngin'."

"I'll see you the end of August."

"Okay," Amanda answered, adding "maybe" as she hung up the phone.

BILL'S RECORD – Chapter Three

Tuesday morning arrived bright and sunny and Summer breezed into the book store about 8:30 a.m.

"Good morning, dear," was Summer's normal greeting.

"Hello on this lovely day!" Kit responded. "Did you open your shop this morning?"

"No. My neighbor's girl, Jainel, will be there this afternoon if need be."

"That is so kind of you. Perhaps we can finish the inventory early."

Kit produced a handwritten notebook comparing the titles to the last records Summer and Bill had prepared.

Summer took a deep breath and let it out slowly when she saw Bill's neat lettering in the columns. How could time go by so fast and drag so slowly at the same time?

Instead of indulging her sorrow, Summer got busy reading the titles aloud while Kit found them on the shelves.

Kit would answer, "here" in response to each title. From time to time she moved the books into alphabetical order.

Summer giggled. "It sounds like students' roll call."

"It does, doesn't it?" Kit looked up and grinned at Summer.

"Are you anxious to get back to teaching?"

"I'm so caught up in things here that I've not thought of it much."

Summer understood and nodded her head. She read another book title.

"Here," Kit replied and moved on.

They had gotten into a good rhythm and were soon finished with the shelves.

"We've been working an hour and a half. Would you like a cup of tea? Kit asked.

"Make it cold with a lot of ice, and I'll say 'yes.'"

"I'll be right back," Kit smiled. Iced tea sounded good to her as well.

Summer put the clipboard on the front counter. Everything was in order according to the lists.

Kit returned with the tea and they sat on the window seat toward the back of the store. After a long sip Kit said, "I've been wondering if perhaps Bill's death was related to his dealing in rare books.

"Nothing valuable is missing according to the inventory," Summer responded. "Besides, I don't think money was the cause of Bill's death. If someone had wanted any of these books, they could have just come in and stolen them when Bill was out fishing, or hiking, or sunbathing."

Kit smiled with the mention of sunbathing but did not comment. "I have another idea. Let's close up and I'll show you Bill's yearbook. I think it may hold some clues – if only I could connect the pieces."

Kit flipped the "open" sign to "closed" and made sure to lock the shop. She and Summer took their glasses of tea up the stairs to the kitchen. Kit brought out the yearbook with the obituaries and the pictures of her brother's old championship basketball team. She refilled their glasses and then opened the book.

Summer felt a shiver go down her back as she saw the team mates "X'd" off, one by one even though she didn't know why they were marked.

"Every one of these players are dead. Bill marked them."

"Bill must have been onto something, Kit. He was not a morbid person, to keep records like this." She fingered the clippings and then came upon Bill's. "Oh."

"Sorry," Kit said and took it from her. "I am the one that numbered the back. It just seemed to fit into the puzzle at the time.

Summer compared the obituaries to the team picture. "Jim Banks, killed that night, pinned under the car in the lake.

He drowned. Sid Tysen, killed in Desert Storm. Matthew Spencer, July 2008, car went off the road and he drowned. Michael Stone, September 2008, drowned in his pool. David Melton, February 2009, electrocuted in his bathtub. Bill Bates, drown in the lake June 2010.

"Do you see that, with the exception of Sid Tysen, these deaths are all water related?"

Kit's eyes grew wider as Summer listed the deaths. "You're right. That's odd."

"Perhaps."

The phone ringing jolted the women back from theorizing about the deaths.

"Bates Books," Kit answered. "Yes, I'm looking forward to it. See you then, Tyler. Good bye." Kit was aware that her cheeks were burning as she hung up the receiver.

Kit's reaction was not lost to Summer. "I don't mean to be intrusive, but was that Tyler Stone you were talking to?"

"Yes. He was a good friend of my family. He was also on the basketball team, see." She pointed to his picture.

"You've said he isn't being very helpful about your suspicions," Summer said.

"That's right. I can't figure him out. One minute I think he's going to agree with me and the next I feel he thinks I am just a foolish little girl that can't cope with my brother's death."

"Tyler is a complicated man. Bill and I enjoyed his company. I know him to be kind and giving. I have also seen him in action – businesslike and unyielding. The three of us were walking home from the street carnival last summer, and a teenager came at us with a baseball bat."

"What?" Kit asked in shock.

"The boy was stoned and he thought we were going to kill him. Tyler disarmed him and had him handcuffed before Bill or I knew what was going on. I was actually in awe of him for a while after that."

"Mom and I were told that there is a drug problem in the area. I also heard that from an old friend."

"Unfortunately, yes. It has consumed so much of Tyler's time. He is on a county wide committee and a state investigative commission to clean up the area's illegal trafficking. It's thought that a lot is being brought in from Mexico."

"Through the work exchange? I thought the program kept a tight reign on the workers."

"Hmmm, perhaps. I wouldn't give much credence to anything you hear, Kit. I don't entirely trust the head of that program."

Kit remembered that Jennifer said that Tyler worked closely with the labor boss. Curious. "The whole thing keeps Tyler away from Kensington, doesn't it?"

"Well, not entirely. If anyone can get to the source, Tyler will."

Kit sat speechless. Of course his work would put him in danger many times, and he would have to be prepared for all sorts of circumstances.

"Kit," Summer asked. "Are you attracted to our illustrious sheriff?"

Kit met her friend's eyes. "I used to have a crush on him and the same old hormones seem to be acting up, but with some of the things Tom has said about his brother, I've been leery of trusting him."

"Well, Tom is an unusual person. Since our discussion on wines the first month I arrived here he has avoided me."

"I noticed he seems to think he knows a great deal about wines."

"Well, he thought his knowledge to be more than a mere farmer's wife."

"You owned a commercial vineyard though," Kit said.

"Ah, but Tom did not understand that. Nor did he know the magnificent wines we made. The Michigan wineries are the main reason I came here in the first place."

"I see," Kit said.

"Tom fancies himself as quite a catch. Monica has been fishing for him for quite a while," Summer stated, "and that's as catty as I'll get."

"Hmmm. He must not be too interested in her with the way he's been coming on to me," Kit mused.

"Half of the eligible women in Kensington want Tyler and the other half want Tom," laughed Summer.

"Well, I have a dinner date with Tyler on Wednesday night," Kit responded. "Do you suppose some of the letters or calls could be coming from jealous women?"

Summer shrugged her shoulders. "Perhaps, but they wouldn't be related to Bill's death, nor would they be life threatening."

"True."

"Since the inventory is done, I'm not going to open the Spinner today. I'm going camping," Summer announced. "Are you coming with me?"

Kit shook her head "no" and walked downstairs and through the shop with her friend. She unlocked the door for Summer and noticed the noon sun shining on Summer's long, auburn hair as she walked away. Kit became depressed, realizing her brother's death had brought sorrow in more ways than one. The phone rang and Kit absent mindedly answered it.

The music in the background was blaring but a person did not answer at first. It angered Kit. "You gutless wonder. We're going to catch you!"

The background became quieter as if the person shut the door on a pay phone booth. "You're next," was the deep, breathy voice's answer.

Kit slammed the receiver down. She decided to keep the book store closed for the rest of the day. She checked to make sure the shop door was locked and then ran up the stairs to double check the back door in the kitchen. She carefully gathered her brother's yearbook together and put it away. The murderer had declared war and she was going to have to be one step ahead of him. She felt very alone and a cold chill went down her spine. She dialed Summer's phone number from the upstairs extension.

"Mystic Spinner."

"So, what does one pack for an overnight at a nudist colony?"

"Nothing," came Summer's gentle voice. "I have everything you'll need. Can you be ready in a half-hour?"

"Right," Kit answered, still shivering.

"I'll pick you up," Summer replied.

Kit sat down heavily at the table, still holding the phone receiver. "A nudist colony," she thought. "Am I that scared to be alone that I'd go to a nudist colony?"

Summer drove up to the rear entrance within the half-hour and Kit, carrying a bag of personal items, double checked the lock as she let herself out.

"I don't know why I'm doing this," Kit ventured as she climbed in the jeep.

"Because it is the right time." Summer smiled. "Social nudity is so misunderstood by the general public, Kit. It is not about exhibitionism, nor is it sexually oriented. A friend of mine wrote a book, 'Naked Before God.' Perhaps you'd want to read it sometime. It's about the nude experience." Summer didn't say anything further, being open to answer any other questions Kit might have.

"I had no idea Bill went to a nudist colony."

Kit, we're not ants. Sun Harbor is a resort with a lot of recreation and a gourmet chef, a great masseuse, and about 80 wooded acres. There is a clubhouse, and oh, just wait 'til you see it all. You'll love it."

"I have to admit I'm curious. I've thought one would have to be pretty open to be a nudist."

"It's all about self acceptance, Kit. People there are pretty healthy about accepting their bodies as natural. You'll be pleasantly surprised at the attitudes of the members."

"Am I going to know any of these people?" Kit asked a little uneasy all of a sudden.

"Probably, but I'll let you learn about the members from themselves."

"Well, I think the real reason I'm with you tonight is that I got another phone call. It frightened me."

Summer slowed her jeep. "Oh, Kit. Are you sure you're strong enough for all of this?"

"If I can go naked, I can be strong enough for anything!" she laughed.

"Social nudity isn't the panacea, it's just the door to discovery."

"Discovery?"

"Yes, of self, of hidden attitudes, of issues. It's amazing what nude meditation at the edge of a lake will do to one's psyche."

"I'm not sure I'll get out of the car."

"Well, it's totally clothing optional, my dear. You can stay clothed if you want. It's all up to you."

Kit sighed heavily. She hadn't realized in running from the fear of being alone she was running into the fear of accepting herself.

The visitor's center was quiet and Summer introduced Kit to Annie. "I'm so very glad you decided to visit. I'll show you a short film that will tell you more about social nudity."

"Go ahead," Summer said. "I'll talk to Della & Marnie while you are watching the film. Kit followed Annie to a comfortable room where a television had been set up. Annie popped a tape in the VCR and then sat down with Kit to watch. Afterwards Kit understood the concept of the park, even though she still wasn't sure she was open-minded enough to participate. She kept hearing the joke playing about in her mind that if God wanted us to go naked, He would have made us that way.

Summer drove through the park at the mandatory nine miles an hour. They drove through the primitive tenting area, and along the lagoon. People in various stages of dress were playing volleyball, miniature golf, walking, riding in golf carts and just soaking up the sun along the water's edge. "See, the lagoon is hidden from the public part of the lake. If you want to go out on the lake, you'll have to be dressed."

It was then that Kit noticed that all of the people on the beach were nude. When the office crew had been totally dressed she almost forgot this was a nudist colony, no, "resort," she corrected herself.

Summer waved to a few people and Kit noted how casual they all were with nudity. Eventually they arrived at the permanent trailer sites. Summer parked beside one and said, "Here 'tis. Trailer Sweet Trailer!"

Seeing the television antenna on the roof Kit remarked, "Now that's what I call roughing it." She smiled and climbed out of the jeep.

"This is my permanent residence. I have a little place behind the Spinner if I need to stay overnight."

"So you actually live here?"

"Yes. Year-round. Come on in. It's known as a park model."

Summer opened all of the windows. Kit brought her overnight bag in and looked around. There were several pictures of Summer and Bill and other friends, some au natural. She blushed in spite of herself.

"You'll get used to it, but go at your own pace. One of the things Bill and I discussed is the fact that physical nakedness is often a stumbling block instead of a stepping stone to spiritual nakedness. It's having the awareness that when you're open to the Creator, that you can be open with yourself and with others. Oh, I could go on and on," Summer laughed. "I'll leave you to yourself while I go sun bathe." Summer went down the hallway and into one of the rooms, but did not close the door. "You can have the other room for yourself. Come down to the beach if you want." She reappeared nude, with a towel draped over her arm. "No swim suits allowed in the lagoon or pool," she smiled and walked out of the trailer.

Kit watched her friend walk toward the beach. She was so nonchalant. Kit went into the second bedroom and undressed. She looked at herself in the mirror. She was a little overweight. She thought her eyes were too large and perhaps she should have a new hairstyle. But, all in all, she liked herself. She understood that the real Kathryn was more than just the fleshly body that stood before the mirror. It was what was in her heart, her spirit, her mind that counted. It was truly that part of her she liked. Still, she had grown up a victim of societal clothing standards. She chuckled to herself as she thought of herself as a victim of fashion. Maybe the atmosphere was liberating her mind already.

She wrapped herself in the large towel she saw on the bureau and went into the living area again. She wanted to ignore the pictures but she wondered if she knew any of the people. Scanning their faces on a group picture she almost dropped the frame. There was no mistaking the man standing next to Summer and Bill – Tyler Stone.

While walking toward the beach she rehearsed how she was going to ask Summer why she didn't tell her the sheriff was a nudist. She met several couples; some had children with them. Many were totally nude, but some had towels or fancy scarves wrapped about them. She then understood what clothing optional meant. She struggled, at first, to look only at the smiling faces that greeted her, and by the time she joined Summer on the beach she was taken with the way everyone seemed so happy.

"I've never seen such beautiful eyes," Kit said quietly when Summer greeted her.

"It's the freedom to be who you are," Summer grinned. "Come on, Kit, meet Joan and Pete."

"Hello, Kit," Joan smiled. "Welcome to Sun Harbor."

"Hope you have a good time," Pete added.

Kit shook hands with both of them and then sat on the lounge next to Summer.

"We're sure sorry about your brother. Bill was a good friend of ours."

"Thank you. I believe I saw you at his funeral."

"That's right. I'm surprised you recognized us," Joan said.

Kit looked puzzled.

"We had clothes on," Joan laughed. "Old joke!"

"I feel like I've landed on a different planet." Kit shook her head.

"Well, just try to relax. We're one big family here," Pete reassured her.

"Why not take a snooze in the shade?" Summer asked. "You'll need sun screen if you stay in the sun."

"Actually, I thought I'd go back to the trailer and take a nap, if you don't mind."

"That's great. Do whatever is comfortable for you."

"Thanks. I want to talk with you later about some pictures I saw." She turned to the other couple. "I hope to see more of you, I mean, see you again." Pete and Joan laughed.

"Talk with you again," Joan replied.

Summer stood up. "I'll walk a ways with you." When they were out of earshot she said, "I told you you'd have some surprises here."

"I had no idea."

"I forgot about the picture. I was going to take it down as I thought it best that Tyler tells you he's a member here."

"What does the town council say about this, I mean, nudity is still frowned upon by a lot of people."

"Right," Summer stopped walking. "And I told you that Tyler is a complicated man. He is very much respected for his work, but he also has a right to a private life."

"True."

"I'll see you later," Summer smiled and walked back to the beach.

Kit slept fitfully for about six hours. During that time Summer had looked in on her twice. She had been concerned that the stress caused by the threats had been bothering Kit.

She left her a note saying she would be up at the clubhouse if Kit wanted to find her.

When Kit finally awakened it took a while to get oriented to where she was. The sun was going down and she stretched, wrapped up in the towel once again and stepped outside. She was on the far side of the lagoon, away from the beach. She walked along the water's edge, the sand squishing up between her toes. The cool water lapping about her ankles made her long to go for a swim. Kit watched the breeze dance across the lake. It created sparkling diamonds on the water. It was a sight she had experienced many times before. However, this time, when the breeze reached her she wanted to feel it on her body. Slowly, she allowed the towel to drop to the ground and she walked into the water up to her ankles. The coolness enveloped her totally and she thought she had never felt such peace.

Kit stood quietly on the shore, being gently caressed by the breeze. It brought her into an awareness that she was a part of the scene that lay before her. She felt one with the earth and the water and the air. She went back and sat on the towel and dug her toes into the sand and her fingers into the grass. Finally, there were no barriers, real or contrived. She sat there feeling connected with something greater than herself. She felt that her inner self was connected with God and nature on a more complete basis. She sat in awe, amazed that she had waited until she was 28 years old to shed her clothes at the edge of a lake. She watched the sun travel beyond the tree line and began to feel the mosquitoes so she reluctantly stood up, picked up the towel, and sauntered back toward the trailer.

She met Summer as she got there and murmured, "I think I'm in love."

Summer smiled broadly. "With whom?"

"With just being here. With the freedom to be me. With all the great feelings I'm feeling."

"I knew you were a natural," Summer said quietly.

"How about dinner? I'm starved!" Kit changed the subject. She didn't want to give Summer the idea that she was adapting too easily.

"Great. Bring your towel to sit on. Dinner is still being served at the clubhouse. My treat."

The two young women walked in the dim light, not afraid of being alone in the country. The clubhouse was brightly lit and music drifted out of the recreation room.

"There's a dance later tonight," Summer told her friend. "But wait until you see what there is for dinner. There is poached salmon, crab meat-stuffed mushroom caps, Caesar salad, fruit, rolls, two kinds of vegetables and carrot cake."

"No greasy hamburgs, eh?"

Well, you could order from the menu."

"This place is too much."

"Sin Harbor?" Summer laughed.

"Paradise Cove might be a better name."

Kit found some security in holding her towel in front of her but found it awkward when choosing her meal. Summer introduced Kit to other friends and they sat down to eat with Jewel, another member there. The three women spoke of the town, Jewel's son being in Afghanistan and the disc jockey, Dale, that would be running the dance that night.

"You can sit with me at the dance if you like. We always have a lot of fun."

Until then she had totally forgot about being nude. "I'm not sure I'm up to a dance," Kit declined, smiling to herself.

"Thanks, Jewel," Summer answered. "Maybe next time."

On the stroll back to the trailer Kit said, "I think I'm getting the idea where spiritual growth is involved."

"Tell me."

"Well, self acceptance is a big issue when working toward growth."

"I believe you will be sorting out your reaction and the results of this visit for weeks to come. It is impossible to understand everything and all the implications at once. When I first experienced the freedom I found being a naturist, I knew it was a healing balm for my weary spirit. That was years ago. When I came to Kensington I missed the social part of nudity and that's why I invested in this place."

"This belongs to you?"

"Not only I. I'm an investor as was Bill. I believe his shares are now in your name."

"I guess I didn't realize it was one of the businesses I inherited. I had no idea Bill was a nudist and now I own a part of the resort?" Kit shook her head in surprise.

"That's right."

They arrived at the trailer and Summer put some water on to boil and continued the conversation. "Bill was in the lifestyle, social nudity, before I moved to Kensington. He said that knowing the truth about yourself sets you free to learn and grow. He embraced that freedom."

"I'm sure it helped to share that viewpoint."

"That we did. We spent a lot of our time here." She made two cups of tea.

"Well," Kit responded as she accepted the cranberry tea, "believe it or not, I can't imagine life without spending time out here."

Summer smiled and touched her friend's arm. "I know."

The women were up early and taking a dip in the lagoon when one of the caretakers came to the beach. Summer called "Good Morning!" to him. He tipped his hat and began emptying trash cans.

"I feel sort of funny with all of the workmen dressed," Kit commented.

"Their clothes are only for protection. I wonder if Geoff saw anything strange on the lake when Bill died."

A man from the lagoon walked by and saluted Geoff and he returned a snappy salute as well "Geoff," Summer called out. "Got a minute?"

Geoff stopped and stood by the trash cans as Summer made her way out of the water. Kit was still amazed at how Summer didn't need the security of a towel as she approached Geoff.

Kit stopped to scoop up both towels, wrapped herself and then caught up to Summer.

Summer, deep into conversation, absentmindedly took the extra towel from Kit and thanked her. "You don't say?" she was commenting to Geoff. A couple of youngsters ran by but stopped to salute the old caretaker. Kit chuckled to see one of the little boys use the wrong hand. Geoff once again returned a quick salute and the boys ran on. "Geoff, this is Bill's sister, Kit. Kit, Geoff."

Geoff nodded to Kit but kept his attention on Summer. "That's right. I was out fishin' a couple hours after dark the night before Bill came up drowned. While I was headin' back to the lagoon my battery ran low and my runnin' lights was out. I seen the sheriff patrol boat on the north side of the lake."

"They didn't see you?" Summer asked.

"Nope. Don't think so. Them lights was out plus I kept real quiet. I heard a funny splash -- like someone slippin' into the water. Thought mebbe they was doin' some skinny dippin'. Then the patrol boat left."

"Could it have been a body being put into the water?" Kit asked almost breathless.

Geoff turned toward her. "Never gave it a thought, missy. Skinny dippin' most likely." He turned back toward Summer who smiled at him.

"You didn't hear any more swimming though. What do you think, Geoff?"

"I think I said enough. I don't want to get involved in any hijinx especially when I ain't got a fishin' license."

Kit started to say something and Summer touched her arm. "Don't worry. We won't say a thing," Summer promised. She gave Kit a stern look that meant to not talk and ushered her away from the old gentleman.

Kit was confused. "Summer," she seethed, "the old man must have been a witness to Bill's being dumped into the lake."

"We know that. Geoff doesn't. I'm afraid he would have had to have a clear view, and so forth to stand up in court."

"But he recognized the patrol boat!"

"In this town that doesn't mean anything. Anyone could have taken the boat out, but it's important information for us to have. Are you ready for breakfast? The kitchen should be open by now."

Kit took a deep breath and let it out slowly. "I suppose you're right." She watched Geoff put the full trash bags into the back of his pick up truck. "Why are people saluting him? Is he retired from the armed services?"

Summer smiled broadly. "See his truck? It's sort of like a family joke here." Geoff drove by and Kit read the side. On the door was painted "General Hauling – Trash Pick Up our Specialty."

"That's too much!" she shook her head and laughed. "They are saluting 'General Hauling'."

"You got it," Summer giggled.

"Okay, let's go eat. Being in the open air gives me quite an appetite."

Most of the resort guests were still asleep at this early hour, having partied late into the night. They ordered breakfast and then looked for a place to sit.

"The Waldens are here!" exclaimed Kit.

"Oh, you know them?" Summer asked.

"Yes, they helped me move into the store."

The women walked toward the couple and Gus stood up and nodded to them. Elly smiled and said, "Have a seat!"

Summer said to Kit, "Elly and Gus have a year-round cottage here."

"I can't imagine what it is like here during the winter. Isn't it too cold to be nude?"

Elly laughed. "Well, we wear coats outside, my dear, but the clubhouse is heated to about 85 degrees and it is very comfortable."

"We go cross-country skiing and warm up by the fire or in the hot tub," chimed in Gus.

"Kit, maybe you'd like to hot tub or go for another swim in the lagoon after breakfast," Summer suggested. "Or, you have a massage!"

"Sure, why not do the whole treatment your first time here?" Elly smiled.

"It all sounds good," Kit responded. Being away from the book store was helping clear her mind.

Over breakfast the foursome discussed Bill and his involvement with the resort and how well-respected he was. Kit wanted to ask about the sheriff but thought it might be too obvious to do so. The massage therapist came in for breakfast and Summer called her over.

"Julia, this is Kit. It's her first time at Sun Harbor. Do you have time this morning to give her a massage?"

"Hi, Kit," Julia grinned. "Congratulations for trying the lifestyle. I'd be ready at 11 o'clock if you'd like a massage."

"Hello, Julia. It sounds wonderful. Where are you located?"

"Near the beach under the stand of white birches."

"Great. I'll be there."

Julia nodded, "Okay see you then," and walked toward the breakfast bar.

"Well, what'll it be?" Summer asked. "I'd like to get some sun before we go back to town."

"Sun it is," Kit responded. "Glad to talk with you again," she said to Elly and Gus. "I have appreciated your help."

"Glad to see you here," the couple almost chimed together.

"Have a relaxing morning," Elly added.

"Thank you. I will," Kit said and she and Summer left the dining room.

They walked toward the beach quietly but Kit was surprised to see the beach filled with sun bathers. "Wow. Where did all of those people come from?"

Summer laughed. "From tents and trailers, my dear. They're going to be soaking up El Sol while he's here."

The women spread their large towels on the lounges and Summer offered some sun screen to Kit. She helped her with her back and then Kit did likewise for Summer. After a few minutes they were ready for the warm sun's rays.

"I've noticed that nudity hasn't stopped anyone from doing anything around here, except maybe the trash pickup."

"Maybe you'll have time for a game of mud volleyball before we leave," Summer said.

"I think not," Kit laughed. For a few minutes she relaxed, soaking up the warmth of the sun, thinking she might actually get used to this feeling. She heard a discussion not far from her, strained to understand the words, but could not. She sat up and looked toward the voices.

"Summer, what's going on over there?"

Summer slipped her sun glasses off her eyes and with one eye looked toward the voices as well. She lay back and said, "That's Dan. He's a teacher and lecturer. He leads workshops on nudism. That's probably one of his groups; reminds me of a guru."

"A nude guru," Kit said. She smiled at Summer.

Summer popped up off the chair in an instant and said, "Come on, you should meet Dan."

Kit was stunned. She really didn't want to approach a group of strangers, but not wanting to be left alone on the beach she got up and followed Summer.

"... so the effects will be far reaching. As the level of understanding is obtained," Dan was saying as the women approached. "You'll be processing your reactions for months to come."

"Hi, Summer!" Dan rose and hugged her. "Everyone, this is my good friend, Summer."

"Greetings everyone," Summer smiled, "and welcome to Sun Harbor. This is my new friend, Kit."

The group shook hands with Summer and Kit and each told the women their names. "Feel free to join us," a heavy-set woman named Jean said. Before they could say anything another person left the group and drew up two more chairs.

"This is the adult fellowship of a nearby church," began Dan as they all sat down again. "They had been studying various aspects of spirituality and I was asked to do a workshop on nudity."

"What does the pastor say about all of this?" Kit asked.

A few giggles came from the group and Jean, the pastor answered. "Well, if I hadn't been convinced that a special connection could be obtained when you stand naked before our Creator, I would have pronounced Dan a charlatan."

"Naked Before God." Dan smiled. "What a person learns is that once you are open and free to be who you are, those traits are magnified."

Kit made the connection that Dan was the author of the book Summer had mentioned yesterday.

Dan continued, "And the best way to approach anything new is without expectation and with an open mind." Nudist parks are no different sociologically than any other place, except there is a freedom to be yourself. People, with pure intentions will seek purity. People with perverse intentions will seek perversion."

"You get out of it what you put into it," responded the young man nodding.

"That's pretty simplified, but accurate."

Kit was distracted by Geoff driving by in a golf cart. Her mind immediately flew to Geoff's statement that he had seen the sheriff's patrol boat out on the lake the night of Bill's murder. Kit shivered despite the warmth of the morning sun. She couldn't concentrate on what was being said. Aware she had suspected her brother's death to be murder before this, she was thoroughly convinced now that it was not accidental.

REINFORCEMENTS – Chapter Four

Kit and Summer strolled back to their lounges. They generously covered every part of their skin that they could reach by themselves, with sun tan lotion. Helping each other protect their backs as well brought giggles. Kit felt warmed by the attitude of the people at Sun Harbor as well as by the sun. After an hour, the women reluctantly trudged to the lodge to use the bathroom and take a break from the sunbathing. They had some iced tea and then Kit returned to the beach for her relaxation massage. Summer joined Dan's group again.

Kit thought it strange, at first, to have a massage session in front of everyone at the lagoon. It also was the first time she was nude for a massage and not covered with a sheet; and with a nude masseuse, no less! Soon she overcame her timidity, listening to the noises around her and realizing from the conversations that no one was paying any attention to her. The smooth gliding movements, feeling catered to, and the soft music playing beneath the table helped her relax further. Her thoughts calmed. Gaining inner contentment, she came to realize she would have to be patient until all the puzzle pieces of the investigation would be found.

Kit and Summer picnicked at the trailer after the massage. It might have been her imagination, but the boiled eggs, cheese, and cut veggies had never tasted better to Kit. "Must be the open air," Kit laughed.

"What's that?" Summer asked.

"Everything is just," and Kit hesitated.

"More natural?" Summer smiled.

All too soon it was two o'clock; and they were packing to return to town that Wednesday afternoon. "Thank you, Summer. It has been an unusual and wonderful experience," Kit said they stopped at the book store's front entrance.

"You're invited any time you'd like to go," Summer replied.

"Thanks," Kit smiled and unlocked the shop. Waving to Summer as she drove away, Kit went in and dropped her bag on the counter and went through the mail. She filled the two orders that had come in. Then she went upstairs, showered quickly and dressed in shorts and a top. She dropped the orders off at the post office and then stopped at the sheriff's office. Kit's first step was to find out who was in charge of the patrol boat the night Bill died.

"Good afternoon, Kathryn," Mary said. The secretary was a woman in her mid-fifties.

"Hello, Mary. How are things going in town without the sheriff here?" Kit tried to make the conversation light.

"Oh, we get along okay," Mary said. "Actually," and she paused, "he's doing some paper work in his office if you want to talk with him."

Kit answered, "I don't need to see him. Actually, I came to ask you a big favor."

"As long as it's legal," Mary replied sternly and then paid close attention.

"I think so. But it will have to be in strict confidence between you and me."

Mary, thinking she would be privy to some juicy gossip made an "X" over her heart and said, "Cross my heart!"

"I'd like to use the patrol boat to see the lake," Kit began.

"Sorry, Kathryn." Mary said, disappointed there was no gossip. "That's not my decision. Tyler even makes the deputies log in and out."

"Really?" Kit's mind raced. "What about the sheriff?"

Mary looked at her strangely and Kit hurriedly said, "Just kidding," and laughed. "Well, I guess I'll just have to rent a boat. See you around!"

"Bye, Kathryn," Mary said. She returned to her paper work.

Kit went to Summer's shop and told her what she had learned. "I need to see that log."

"Kit, perhaps you'd better let Tyler handle this." Summer shook her head.

"I can't."

"Surely you don't suspect Tyler?" Summer stated surprised.

"I feel confused at times," Kit admitted. "May I use your jeep?"

Summer handed her the keys. "Be careful."

"I will. Thanks." It took a few minutes to get used to the manual transmission, but soon she was driving with a little difficulty. Kit drove the short distance to park where the patrol boat was moored. She was relieved to see it was not there. She parked behind the small office, out of view of the rest of the park and tried the side door first and then the window and found them both locked. There was no one there. The large windows, facing the lake were open and she saw how easily she could remove the screens. While she was debating whether or not she could climb in without being seen by the people on the beach, the patrol boat pulled up to the dock. She waved to the deputy and received two short boat horn toots in response.

The deputy swung over the side, tied the boat to the mooring post, and walked toward Kit.

"Afternoon, Ms. Bates. What brings you out this way?"

"Afternoon, Carl. I thought somewhat of taking a boat ride and couldn't remember who rented boats and ..."

"Sheppard's across the lake," Carl pointed unlocking the office. He stood in the doorway thinking she would be leaving.

Instead Kit asked, "How's the lake level?"

"Oh, it's down with the lack of rain."

"I guess the weather affects a lot of things," she continued, running out of things to talk with him about.

Finally, he went inside the office. "Excuse me a minute," he said while looking at his watch. He then picked up a ledger and wrote the time down. "Gotta' log out."

Kit followed him inside, backed up against the side window and unlocked the screen. Then, she pretended to be looking at the map on the wall.

"Well," Carl continued, "I'd like to chat, but my patrol is done for today."

Kit felt pretty smug. "Sure. Thanks for the information!" she responded. She bounced out to the jeep and waved to Carl again. Travelling down a side road, she waited until Carl drove by. Parking the car there, she sneaked back to the beach.

The office was deserted now and the only barrier between her and the ledger was the unlocked screen on the side window. Before thinking twice she was inside the office and straining to see the ledger in the late afternoon light. She had to flip back a few pages and finally located the entries on the night Bill drowned. She was stunned to see Tyler's handwriting as the last log out of the day. Kit hurriedly put the ledger back in place, and climbed back through the window, glad that she had worn sports clothes.

Once again her habit of jumping to conclusions made Kit almost run to Summer's jeep. Maybe Summer could help her sort it out. Driving back to her shop she tried to convince herself that the timing was different. Tyler logged out at 9 p.m. Hadn't Geoff said he was out a couple hours after dark? When did it get dark anyway?

Kit parked Summer's jeep behind the Spinner and returned her keys. "You're never going to believe what I did."

"Probably not."

"I went to the patrol boat office, waited until Carl left, and got a look at the log."

"How did you manage that?"

"Climbed through the window."

"You actually broke into a law enforcement office?" Summer asked. Kit shook her head "yes" and Summer laughed. "Well, I'll give you credit for intestinal strength; the intelligence quotient has dropped a level however."

"Oh, Summer, I just had to know about Tyler. He logged out at 9 p.m."

"All the log tells you is he logged out at 9 p.m. It gets dark later than that time, so it couldn't have been him in the patrol boat later when Geoff saw it."

"I know. It makes me feel better about Tyler; unless Geoff was wrong."

"Kit," said Summer shaking her head. "What made you think someone using the boat would log in? Tyler could have gone back and used it later as well as anyone else on the lake having access to the boat."

Kit sighed heavily. "I'm not thinking straight."

"Go home, get ready for your dinner with Tyler, and forget this whole thing for a while."

Kit hugged Summer. "You're right. Thanks for being a friend." Kit dragged herself back to the book store. What was she doing?

Kit decided she was on overload. She needed the dinner with Tyler to distract her and thought about the positive influence Summer had become in her life. She wondered how Tyler would feel about her having a partnership with Summer. Tom certainly didn't have any use for her. Did Tyler's opinion really matter that much? Yes, she decided, as she climbed into the hot shower. She took pains to dress carefully because everything had to be just right when he picked her up. Why? she kept asking herself as her stomach began to tie up into a knot. He might be just as much a suspect as anyone else. Could she still have those feelings of love for him? No, the other time she felt this way about him was ten years ago and she had been a child.

Before she realized, it was almost 7:30 and she was assessing her appearance in the bedroom mirror. At the last minute, she removed the jacket of her suit and replaced it with a sweater shawl. Not quite so formal, she mused.

Tyler knocked at the back door promptly at 7:30. It was a surprise to see him casually attired, for even the day of the funeral he had been in uniform. "Off duty, Sheriff?" she teased.

"Yes, ma'am. It's about time some of my deputies do the extra hours." He checked to see that the door was locked behind them. As they left, Tyler offered her his arm, and tapped at the wind chimes. The wooden pieces pealed all the way down the stairs.

Kit smiled slightly. He always made her feel special. He opened the LeBaron's door and she was enveloped with the sweet cherry blend tobacco aroma again. She had totally missed this the night of Bill's funeral.

He walked around and as he got in he reached to the back seat and produced a small flower that Kit recognized as an orchid. "It's a cymbidium hybrid; grew it myself," he said as he offered it to her.

"It's so delicate, thank you." She tucked it behind her ear and asked, "How's that?"

"Lovely." He smiled, looking into her eyes.

Kit met his gaze, knowing he did not speak of the flower, and she felt herself blushing and glad that it was twilight.

He started the car and drove down the alley. "How are the book sales?"

"Doing well. Summer and I have been talking about the store. She may help me."

"That sounds good. She's a fine person."

Kit noted Tyler's opinion of Summer differed from Tom's. Suddenly she thought the area looked familiar so she asked, "Isn't this your street?"

"Yes. I couldn't decide where to go tonight so I'm going to do the cooking." He turned into his driveway and pushed the button on the garage door opener on the dashboard. The door began to lift and Tyler drove in. The door closed behind them, creating a womb-like atmosphere.

"You certainly are a man of many talents, Mr. Sheriff!" Kit giggled as he helped her from the car.

He held the door to the breezeway open and said, "My home is your home, Ma'am."

Kit flounced past him and saw the patio lights glowing cheerfully around the pool.

"I thought we could eat on the patio; that is if you don't mind."

"Mind?" Kit answered. "This brings back some wonderful memories," she laughed. "After Mom and Dad divorced, your home became a special place for Dad and Bill and I."

"We did have some good times together. Now Mike, your dad and brother are gone," Tyler said wistfully.

"You still have Tom and me," Kit grinned.

Tyler chuckled. "Tom is gone for the weekend. He left about an hour ago. Make yourself comfortable. I'll be right back." Tyler went into the house.

Kit strolled about the pool area and watched as Tyler put steaks on the gas grill. She stared at the rising moon's reflection in the water and shuddered. The thought of Mike Stone drowning in this pool was upsetting. She had heard that Tom had found him.

Kit noticed a glow coming from inside the greenhouse and she stopped and peered in. Tyler startled her as he said from behind her, "There's a light switch just inside to your left."

"Do you mind if I look?"

"No, of course not. It's still a favorite hobby of mine after all of these years."

The smell of the warm earth and foliage enveloped her as Kit stepped in. She found the light switch and then caught her breath at the sight of hundreds of blossoms. "Oh, they're lovely; just as I remembered." Kit smiled.

Tyler came up behind her and stood in the green house doorway. "I never get tired of babying them," Tyler answered.

"I feel like I'm in a jungle paradise," Kit walked further into the greenhouse but stopped walking as she saw the mangled black orchid plant on the potting table. "What on earth?"

Tyler's mood changed rapidly. "A neighborhood dog got in here last week and broke a few plants. I'm trying to save this one because I've had it for so long."

Kit paled as she recognized the blooms as identical to the one that was in the flower arrangement she received; the one with large thorns and a threatening note. "How?" she managed to ask, trying to hide her shock of the discovery.

"Can't figure it out. I was sure I'd closed the door."

She looked up again at Tyler, and he was studying her. "It'll grow back in time. It's a common black."

"That's good," Kit managed, and she turned to leave the greenhouse. Perhaps she was just letting her mind get away from her. Even Tom said the black orchid could have come from anywhere.

"Staying here was a nice idea, Tyler. I'd rather talk in private anyway," Kit said as they walked back to the grill.

Tyler turned the steaks and noted she was being less formal with him. He closed the lid and said, "Is there something special you want to talk about?"

"Yes. It might not be pleasant," she hesitated.

"Let's sit down." They did. "Okay, shoot," he said, giving her his full attention.

"I found an album Bill kept. Actually it was your senior year book. He had saved death notices for each of the members of your basketball team."

Tyler pursed his lips, sat back in the deck chair, and looked at Kit. "Your brother and I spent many hours talking about the team and what happened. The night of the accident was traumatic for all of us. I wouldn't get in the car and tried to keep the other fellas from leaving. A couple of us spent the night on the beach. There's this little hidden cove on the north side."

Kit's stomach felt uneasy when she realized that was the cove where she and Tom had their picnic. She fought to pay attention to Tyler's story.

"Anyway," Tyler continued, "when we woke up in the morning we walked to town. That's when we learned what had happened. For years I felt responsible for not stopping them."

Kit sat quietly knowing the memory was painful for Tyler. He took a deep breath and then asked, "What do you want to know?"

"There are five team members that I wondered about, that is, if you know their whereabouts."

Tyler did not say anything so Kit continued. "The first is Dan Gregory."

"Dan moved to California shortly after graduation. He graduated from U.S.C. and was a teacher the last I heard."

Kit continued, "Pete Jackson."

"Pete married Sally Barton. They live a couple hundred miles from here. He was in a factory accident a couple years back and was blinded."

Kit frowned. "Too bad. How about Burt White?"

"Burt was a real scrapper. He led the team in steals and fights on the court. He was in some trouble and spent time in prison. He was paroled after a year and I've heard nothing about him since."

"Don Milton is another one."

"Don Milton. Let's see now." Tyler bit his lip and watched the tree tops move with the breeze. "We called him 'Milty' because he was funny like Milton Berle. As far as I know he died a couple of years ago, shortly after Mike."

"Where was he living?"

"He was in Florida the last I heard."

"Still alive though?"

"Yes. Anyone else?"

"Tyler Stone."

"Let's see. He's good looking, smart, trustworthy ..."

"... and burns steak." Kit pursed her lips.

Tyler jumped up and rescued their supper.

They ate salad, bread sticks, baked potatoes and grilled steak, all the while talking about the verses in the poetry book Tyler had given Kit.

"I especially liked the poem in the back called "Fantasy Love" where the writer talked about making love with her eyes," Tyler said.

"That really is a fantasy," Kit laughed.

"Don't you think it's possible?" Tyler asked, keeping her gaze.

"Well, I," she stammered.

"It's said that your eyes are the windows to your soul. What do you think?"

"That perhaps it's difficult to know the difference between fantasy and reality at times."

"Coffee's ready." Tyler smiled.

"Great." Kit returned his smile.

"Why do you want to know about the high school team, Kathryn?"

"I'm trying to piece things together," Kit responded and took the cup from Tyler.

"You're still thinking Bill was murdered."

"Tyler, how many times did you go fishing with Bill?"

"Countless."

"Was he ever without his lucky hat?"

"No."

"His death was reported as an accidental drowning – while fishing. His rod was in the boat, but I found his hat hanging on the door in the pantry."

Tyler stared at his coffee cup. He put it on the table and then looked directly at Kit. "And you think one of the remaining five men could be responsible?"

A chill crept up Kit's spine because she realized Tyler Stone was one of those five. "Not you, Tyler!" she said quickly, her eyes large, hoping she was convincing.

"That's a relief," he said. "Would you like to dance?"

"Sure," Kit answered, glad once again that the subject had changed. If he were involved, she did not want him to think she suspected him.

Tyler turned the stereo volume up and took Kit into his arms. They glided around the pool quickly and Kit was impressed with his skill.

A slower love song came on, and Tyler pulled Kit nearer, and she willingly molded herself to his lean body. She breathed in deeply of his spice cologne and beyond that the scent of the man holding her. She became heady with the knowledge that he enjoyed being close to her.

The song ended and they stood beside the pool and looked deeply into one another's eyes, still locked into an embrace. Kit wanted desperately for Tyler to kiss her. The closeness they had just by looking into one another's eyes made her feel more loved than she ever had been.

"Tyler?" she whispered.

Tyler crushed her to himself. How could he explain how much he wanted her – that if he kissed her he would not be able to stop. One night in her arms would never quench this fire. He wanted her forever. He needed her to come to him without reservation, and right now he was afraid she suspected him of her brother's murder. Suddenly dropping his arms, he let go of her and walked back toward the house.

Kit almost lost her balance as Tyler left. Maybe she was fantasizing. She feared he was just playing mind games – hoping she would drop her investigation. She was getting very used to offering up silent prayers for understanding.

"I'll take you home, Kathryn."

Kit hurried to the table and picked up her purse. They drove home in silence. Tyler drove to the front of the store intending to see her to the door.

Suddenly Kit screamed, turned to Tyler and buried her face in his shoulder. Walking in front of him, Kit saw the dead cat first. The cat was hanging by the neck, a note dangling from its tail.

Tyler walked her around the store and to the back entrance. He waited until she was safely inside and said, "I'll be back in a few minutes."

Tyler returned a while later and used the kitchen sink to wash up. Kit was sitting at the table, still shaking. He asked "Are you all right, Kathryn?"

"Not really; what did the sign say?"

"It doesn't matter," he said and locked the door.

"It said, "dead K A T," didn't it?"

Tyler frowned but pulled her to her feet and encircled her in his strong arms. "Maybe you should go home, Kathryn. I don't want for you to be hurt."

"Tyler Stone. You're the sheriff. What are you doing about this?" she demanded, still shaking.

"Calm down. I'll re-open the investigation. Bill always wore his lucky fishing hat."

The full implication of Tyler's decision to reopen the investigation crashed down on Kit. Those really were life threatening calls she had received, and now a dead cat had been hung on her door. She felt weak and swayed toward Tyler. She leaned heavily on him and he was content to comfort her.

"You need some sleep, little girl," he whispered.

Kit felt that tugging deep within that had been growing ever since she returned to Kensington. She wanted more from Tyler than just to be a little girl that he watched over. She moved her hands to the back of his head and pulled his face down to hers. "Don't leave. I don't want to be alone."

Tyler slid his hands to the small of her back and pressed her hips to him, allowing her to feel what her plea was doing to him. "What exactly are you asking?"

Kit brushed her lips softly against Tyler's and he kissed her hesitantly. "Tyler?" she breathed heavily and stroked his back.

Tyler swept her up into his arms and carried her to the bedroom through the darkened apartment, his way shown by the moonlight streaming in the windows, knowing full well that she would be his wife. He put her down beside the bed and held her at arm's length. The moonlight made her ivory skin look silken, and Tyler shuddered with desire.

"Kathryn," Tyler whispered huskily. "I want to make love to you more than do anything else in this world, but I want to make sure it's what you want as well."

Kit settled any remaining doubts Tyler had by pulling him close to her and kissing him passionately. Their tongues reached deeply as if searching for their very souls. He lifted her to the bed carefully and stood next to her unbuttoning his shirt, watching her all the while. She smiled, "You're gorgeous." Tyler chuckled thinking how beautiful she was.

Their eyes met again, and Tyler pulled her to her feet and slowly, hands gliding tenderly, he began the long process of helping her undress. They continued caressing one another gently as they lay upon the bed and Tyler explored her neck and kissed her eyelids and cheeks. He rasped, "You are the beautiful one, Kit. You take my breath away."

Kit also felt it difficult to breathe. Tyler's kisses were soft, and every spot his lips touched was ignited with fiery desire. His sensuous exploration of her body was an eternal journey that she had only thought possible. Was this really happening? She found herself praying that this love was real.

Tyler moved closer and she opened herself to him – not just her body, but her mind and her spirit as well.

In the moonlight their eyes met again and both smiled slightly. Tyler looked deeply into Kit's eyes. He held her firmly against him. "You're mine, Kathryn," he whispered huskily. "You belong to me now."

They kissed deeply and she answered, "Yes, Ty. Yes, I do belong to you."

Tyler's desire for her had not waned over time, but was now being fully expressed because of his love for Kit.

They fell asleep in one another's arms. When Kit awoke they were covered with the quilt that she knew she had not pulled up. Ty was such a caring person, she thought. She used the bathroom and returned to bed and studied Tyler's facial features as he slept. He said that she belonged to him. Did he mean it? She wanted him to possess her, but not own her. If she learned that Tyler killed her brother now it would be devastating.

Tyler was waking up, and she did not want to continue that line of thinking. She followed his strong jaw line with her fingertip until his eyes fluttered open. "Oh, I didn't mean to awaken you."

"Liar," he grinned and wound his fingers into her hair. He drew her closer. "Do you understand how much I love you?"

"Was last night an indication?" she teased.

He kissed her tenderly and the desire to experience the fullness of his love again swept over her. To her surprise however, he sat up and said, "It's almost daylight. I'd better go before the neighbors have something to talk about."

"Please don't leave," Kit coaxed.

Tyler pulled her from the bed. "There will be plenty of time for loving. When will you marry me?"

"What?" Kit asked astonished.

"I don't fool around, Kathryn. Last night was for keeps," he said slowly.

A hundred ideas swirled around in her head – the strongest misgiving that plagued her was her question of his involvement in her brother's murder. "I've loved you for a very long time, Ty, but being in love with you is so new to me."

"I won't let you get away from me." He whispered, his embrace becoming stronger.

There was no denying that she had fallen in love with him. "Ask me again in a while, Tyler. I believe I do love you."

Tyler lifted her off her feet and twirled around laughing. "That's good enough for me," he said as he put her down. "I'll take a shower and get out of here before the neighborhood wakes up." He left her standing there dazed.

Tyler stood under the hot water smiling and thanking God Kit had come back into his life.

Kit slipped into her robe and went to the kitchen to brew the coffee. She poured two glasses of orange juice and set out some strawberries and English muffins.

Tyler soon joined her and said, "I'm going to leave without eating. Kathryn, we have to live in this town, and I don't want to have to overcome gossip. I'm on duty all day today. Can we talk at lunch tomorrow?"

"I may be going to go shopping tomorrow." She had hoped to be able to contact an investigator that day. "How about dinner instead?"

"I didn't want to wait that long," he growled playfully. "I'll pick you up about seven and we can go over to Emerald Harbor Inn. This time you can have squab or anything else you would like."

"How romantic," she smiled.

"It can be." Tyler kissed her long and tenderly, leaving her weak in the knees. He left quietly and she sat down at the table stunned. Live here permanently? She hadn't even considered the idea! Her position and friends ... what would her mother say?

The sun's first rays topped the trees and Kit poured a cup of coffee. She took it into the bathroom and drew a hot bath with plenty of bubbles. As she softly stroked herself with the soapy wash cloth, she thought of Tyler's caresses and she flushed in remembrance of her reaction to him. How long had she been attracted to him without fully understanding?

Kit dressed and called her mother, hoping it wasn't too early. "Good morning," her mother bubbled.

"Hello, Mom."

"Darling, how are you? Are you making enough to pay your bills? Is Tyler Stone taking care of you?"

Kit laughed, wanting to share exactly how much Tyler was taking care of her. "Mother! Slow down."

"Well, it's about time you called!"

"I know, but a lot has been happening. You asked about Ty."

"How is the old dear?"

Kit could feel the color rising. Old? "Well, Mom," Kit hesitated.

"Kathryn!" Amanda commanded. "Spit it out!"

"Tyler asked me to marry him," Kit said, expecting her mother's disapproval.

"I wondered how long it would take him."

"You knew?"

"You didn't?" her mother asked somewhat shocked.

Kit began to cry. "I never thought I'd fall in love again."

"What's the problem?"

"Oh, Mom. I've only been here for two weeks."

"But, my darling girl, you've loved him for years. So, when's the big day?"

"Not for a while. Ty puts a great deal of store in respectability. We haven't even been seen together in public."

Amanda giggled. "Keep me posted."

"I will. Love you, Mom."

"Love you too, sweetheart. Bye."

Kit went downstairs to the shop and took care of a few odds and ends. She picked up the telephone directory and looked in the yellow pages where she had circled "Lou Turney Investigations." It was in Pittford and had looked promising. She dialed the number, hoping to leave a message and was surprised to have the call answered.

"Lou Turney Investigations," came a pleasant, husky female voice.

"Hello. I'd like to speak with Mr. Turney as soon as possible."

"Let's see. Lou has a 1:00 o'clock open tomorrow. Would you like that?"

"Yes. Thank you. My name is Kathryn Anderson, maiden name Bates. Bill Bates from Kensington was my brother."

"Of Bates Books?"

"Yes."

"I'm sorry for your loss. What can I say your appointment will be about?"

"There are too many strange circumstances surrounding Bill's drowning. I would like his death investigated."

"Hmm, I see. Well, I'll write all of this down. I'm sure Lou will be interested in talking with you."

"Thank you. My friend, Summer and I will be there at 1:00 o'clock tomorrow."

"The office is on the third floor of the bank building on Main Street. The entrance door is on the side."

"Okay. Thanks."

"You're welcome. Good bye."

Now that was fortunate, Kit thought. She was very pleased that she would not have to wait long. She and Summer would be speaking with Mr. Turney tomorrow afternoon.

She was going to call her friend when the phone broke the otherwise quiet morning. Steeled not to allow some jerk to spoil her day, she took a deep breath before answering.

"Hi darlin'," Tyler's deep voice boomed. "Just thought I'd take my break with the woman I love!"

Kit shut her eyes as she answered, "Hello, my love. I trust all is peaceful in town."

"We had a hydrant opened and kids playing in the water," but other than that all's well.

"Did you arrest the culprits?"

"No. Watched them play for about 15 minutes before the fire department closed the hydrant. It was a toss up between wasting water and letting kids enjoy themselves."

"I can't remember it ever being this hot here mid-June."

"I seem to remember one summer in '95 or '96," Tyler trailed off. Some shouting was heard in the background and he added quickly, "I gotta' go, Kit."

"Be safe. I love you," Kit started but the line went dead before he could answer.

That's great, she thought. Now I'm going to worry about what's going on.

She turned over the "open" sign and unlocked the front door. The phone rang again. Thinking it was Tyler calling her back she answered in a sexy voice, "Hellooo."

"Nice," growled the caller. "Maybe I won't kill you quickly."

Kit slammed the phone receiver down in the caller's ear. She locked the door and went back upstairs. She brewed some mint tea for later. Finding her note pad she added this phone incident to the list she would be giving to the investigator the next day. She called Summer but her friend wasn't home. Probably at Sun Harbor, she mused.

Kit walked down to the corner store and picked up a newspaper. She decided to look at used vehicles. If she were going to stay in the area, she might as well see what was being offered. She went back home and drank iced mint tea on the back landing as she looked at the used car ads. After a while, she had circled three prospects.

Kit took the newspaper with her to the car lot. Her husband, Gregg, had died in their car and she had not wanted to own one since then. Living in Lansing, it was easy to ride the bus no matter where she needed to go.

"Hello, little lady," the car salesman said.

"Good afternoon."

"Do you have an idea of what you are looking for?" he asked.

She produced the advertisement.

"Well, two of these have sold already. The other one is in sad shape."

"Okay, thanks." She turned to leave.

"Just a minute. A really nice Jeep came in yesterday. Would you like to see it?"

"Sure. It wouldn't hurt to look."

The Jeep was a similar model to the one Summer drove. It needed some body work, it appeared. "Here she is – just needs some tender loving care," the salesman said.

"I tell you what. I will be back to look at it after you administer your 'tender loving care.' If the price is right we may have a deal." Kit smiled. She really liked the Jeep.

"Whooie, you drive a hard bargain. Give me your phone number and I'll call you when it is done."

"Just call Bates' Books and ask for Kathryn."

"Okey dokey! Glad you stopped in.

Kathryn walked back home happy with her bargaining. She still had not said 'yes' but at least the Jeep would be in better shape.

At a few minutes past nine, Tyler called. He was going to come over if it was convenient.

"Of course it is!" Kit almost bubbled. She was happy for the company.

"How about a moonlight swim?" Tyler asked as she opened the door to him.

"Well, it has been hot all day," Kit answered.

"There a place I'd like for you to see," Tyler said as he came into the kitchen.

Kit, teasing him, grasped at her heart and let her eyes grow wild, "Oh, no – Sin Harbor!"

Tyler was stunned. "How did you know?"

"I was there yesterday with Summer."

"Great – then no explanations needed. Wanna' go?"

"Sure. Let me grab some towels." Kit went to the linen closet, stuffed a couple large towels into a rattan tote bag and was back in the kitchen in a jiffy.

Tyler didn't say anything as he opened the door for her and then checked the lock as they left. His level of appreciation for this woman just kept growing every day.

At one point during the ride over Kit started thinking of how each of the team members' deaths was water-related. What if he was going to drown her? Maybe she should fake a sudden headache, or maybe she should not let fear rule her life.

Tyler pulled up in front of a park model. "This is it."

Kit saw that it was only two units away from Summer and that there was a light on there. "Hey, look. Summer is here," she said as she got out of the car. "I'm going to go say hi while you open up."

"Sure. I'll walk over."

Kit walked the short distance quickly and knocked on the door. "Why, Kit, what brings you here?"

"A moonlight swim with Tyler," Kit said.

"Come in. You look terrified."

"I can't help it. All this nonsense about water deaths."

"Oh, my dear friend," Summer began and shook her head sincerely. "You need to let someone like Tyler protect you, not frighten you."

"I'm just confused. I love him and I just don't know what I'd do if he isn't who I think he is."

"Hello in the cabin!" called Tyler from outside.

"Trust him, Kit," Summer smiled as she opened the door. "Ah, and if it isn't our esteemed sheriff standing sky clad before us!"

"Want to join us for a swim?"

"I'd like that," she grabbed a towel, a blanket and motioned Kit to the door.

"I feel positively overdressed," Kit giggled as she joined her two friends walking to the lagoon. By the time they got there, however, she had shed her clothes and was in the water before either of them.

The water in the lagoon was warm but still very refreshing after the heat of the day.

The three of them took turns sighing as they allowed the magic liquid to wash away their emotional fatigue.

"This is exquisite – the way we should all be in nature," Summer said.

"I have to agree," Kit said as she floated with her eyes closed.

Tyler and Summer smiled at each other. Kit was a definite convert.

Walking back to the park model Tyler offered, "We can spend the night here if you wish – as long as we're back in town early."

"I'd like that!" was Kit's response.

"Well, I'll be saying good night. Thanks for the swim!" Summer said and left the two of them in front of Tyler's home.

Their lovemaking was almost meditative. It was slow and so filled with gentleness that Kit thought she might actually be levitating at one point. Then, an urgent passion seized Tyler and he swept Kit up in the frenzy. It excited her beyond anything she'd ever known. Breathless, they stayed tangled in each other's arms and legs, a sweaty heap, for a long while.

Tyler was the one to get up instead of falling asleep that way. Opening a bottle, he asked Kit, "Would you like a beer?"

Kit stretched, took a deep breath and sat up. "Absolutely, thanks." They wrapped up in towels and padded barefoot out to the deck.

Tyler turned the electric bug "zapper" on and spread his towel on the glider. "Join me?"

"The night is still hot," Kit commented as she sat next to him.

They sat quietly, listening to crickets and frogs calling. The almost full moon was mid-sky. "I can't think of anything more peaceful," Tyler sighed.

"Close to Heaven," Kit answered.

"What would make it Heaven?"

Kit turned to him and when he smiled she said, "There. Seeing your smile."

"A bit of a romantic, eh?"

"You bettcha'. How about you? And don't say the same thing," Kit laughed.

"Okay," he answered. "No crime in Kensington; a little idealistic I suppose."

"And how would you bring about world peace?"

Tyler laughed. "The world will have to take care of itself. My only concern is our village."

"Overwhelming?"

"Not really."

"The crime commission in Lansing must be some help."

Tyler took a long tug on the bottle. "How do you know about that?"

"Summer. She says you are well-respected."

He chuckled. "Feared is more like it. People know I'm tough, but fair. I feel responsible for the citizens' well being."

"Drug trafficking?"

Tyler answered, "I'm not the only one dealing with it. Others from the county commission are also investigating."

Kit nodded and Tyler added "I'll do just about anything to keep a tight reign."

Kit wondered what "anything" was to him. "So, do you have big plans for Kensington's future?"

"Not really. We have to live in the present. I'm not going to let anyone get in the way. Even if it means using unconventional means now."

Kit heard his determination to keep the village crime free – but at what cost? And who would "get in the way"?

Five a.m. came very early, and true to Tyler's not wanting to create gossip, he delivered Kit back to her apartment before the town was waking up. Later that morning Kit opened the store and began checking invoices.

The mail was delivered and she sorted advertising from the bills and orders. Kit dealt with the orders first and was delighted at her clients' continued support. Kit opened a manila envelope and its contents fluttered to the floor. Kit recognized it as a Polaroid picture and picked it up and read the back first. "You're next, Kitty Kat." She turned if over slowly, revealing the grotesque picture of the cat that had been hung on her front door. Her stomach churned and she shoved the picture back into the envelope. The bell tinkled behind her and she turned quickly to see Summer white-faced and out of breath. She came in and held the back of a chair for support. "What on Earth is wrong?" Kit asked.

"I was at the newspaper office putting in our ad for this week when an obituary notice came in." She took a deep breath before continuing. "It was for Dan Gregory!"

"Bill's teammate, Dan Gregory?"

"Yes. He and his family were vacationing at his wife's parents' home in Indiana last week. There was a boating accident, and get this, the police have not been able to find the driver of the other boat."

Kit sat down on the high stool behind the counter and held her head in her hands. She looked up and asked, "Last week?"

"We have to keep our wits about us, Kit. I'm going to call Tyler."

The door opened and the sheriff came into the book store just in time to hear Summer's last sentence. "Did I hear my name mentioned?" He grinned but sobered once he saw the women's expressions.

Summer told him about his former teammate and he stood there quietly, shaking his head. Kit watched him for any kind of strange reaction, but none came.

"Don't leave Kit alone today, Summer," Tyler said seriously. He turned to Kit. "I'm going to make some phone calls and will talk with you this evening." Kit nodded and Tyler strode out of the shop. She watched him walk up the street and Summer came to her side.

"He's worried about your safety." Summer began.

"Ty was gone during the time Dan Gregory was killed, and after what Tom has told me," Kit blurted out, "I'm beginning to be afraid of the man I've fallen in love with!"

"Kit, I can't believe Tyler Stone murdered Bill, or any of the other men for that matter." Summer put her hand on Kit's shoulder.

"I hope Tyler comes up with some solid evidence against someone else pretty soon. I'm beginning to question my ability to think straight where he is concerned."

"Well, fear is a deceiver, Kit. Don't allow any kind of fear to cloud your thinking."

Kit met her eyes and saw an intensity she understood. Hadn't she been thinking the same thing? "You're right," and changing the subject said "Can we lighten the mood and take our lunch early? All this stress makes me hungry."

Summer relaxed and thought there were several things that made Kit hungry. "Sure, where to?"

"Do you mind driving?"

"That's fine, I'll get the Jeep," Summer answered and went to the door. "I'll be back in about a half hour. You'll be okay, won't you?"

"Of course. I'll meet you out front." Kit locked the door behind her as Summer left. She gathered her large tote bag that was already packed with her note pad and Bill's newspaper clippings and put it on the counter. Then she ran upstairs, checked her appearance, and was out in front of the shop, tote in hand by the time Summer returned.

"I'd like to go to Pittford. They have a mean pizza place."

"This isn't about pizza," Summer responded.

"How very clever of you. Pizza's just the excuse. I'm hungry for information and there's a certain Mr. Lou Turney there."

"That owns an investigation firm? That would be Ms. Louise Turney."

"Oh, that was probably her yesterday. She had a rather deep voice." Before Summer could comment, Kit commented, "And, oh, by the way, you're right," Kit began.

"About what?"

"About thinking there are a lot of things that make me hungry, like the open air, stress, working on an empty stomach."

Summer looked away from the road long enough to look at Kit questioningly.

"I saw your look when I said I was hungry," Kit offered without Summer saying anything.

"So, you read facial reactions?" Summer smiled as she looked back to the road.

"Sure, and I see one very smug lady right now."

"You're right. I told you that you are spiritually sensitive. You'll enjoy meeting Lou."

Pittford was an ethnically diverse city of 72,000, mainly due to the university and junior college. Their campuses were tucked among the rolling hills; even so, the city fathers kept a close watch on the students. The school population swelled on league game weekends for both basketball and football, although the summer semester found many of the dormitories empty.

"Tyler told me there is a good anti-drug task force here," Summer said as they came into town.

"Part of the state commission I suppose."

"Yes, I think they are close to finding the source of the problem."

"Bracero bosses? Local businessmen?" Kit asked.

"Possibly both," Summer agreed.

As they came into the inner city, the women noted street corners dotted with various types of young adults and teens.

"Looks like we're in the 'student ghetto' here," Kit said.

"Yes, they've always called it that. It's just student housing in the older part of the city."

As if on cue, as they went by a large house, a young man started running down the steps of the porch and right toward the road. Summer put on the brakes swiftly without slamming her foot down. Another young man started chasing the runner, and they veered out of the path of the Jeep just in time.

"Good grief!" Kit exclaimed. As quickly as she said that, a short blast from a police siren sounded behind them.

The Jeep was at a standstill by then and the police tore out around them with lights flashing. The squad car overtook and pulled up in front of the running students causing them to almost run into the car. In a flash, the doors of the squad car flew open and both officers were out. The students didn't attempt to run and as rapidly as it began the chase was over.

"I didn't even know they were there," Summer uttered under her breath as she started past the police commotion.

"Oh, it looks like they've found something," Kit said as she craned her neck while they passed by.

"And that's why Tyler and his deputies train so often."

A large black sedan with darkened windows was on the next corner slowly pulling away. "Oooooo," Kit joked, "that looks ominous! I thought tinted windows were illegal in Michigan." As they came closer she added, "New Mexico plates. It's just like the car parked outside of Monique's so often."

"Maybe they're dealers," Summer said. "Write their plate number down. We'll tell Tyler about it."

Kit scrambled for some paper and wrote down the license plate numbers and shoved it back into her purse. "There's the pizza place I told you about."

Summer maneuvered the Jeep into the parking lot which had several student-aged patrons sitting at the stone picnic tables out front. "Let's get our pie to go and we can sit in the park," she suggested.

"Good idea," Kit answered as she climbed out of the Jeep. They ordered and then waited for about 15 minutes watching the other customers. "Were we ever that young and carefree?" Kit asked.

"No. I was going on 40 when I turned 10," Summer said wistfully.

Kit didn't follow her friend's comment because the waiter called her name to pick up their pizza.

It was a short ride to Alamo Park, and the women found a small wooden picnic table at the edge of the fountain. "Love this double cheese," Kit smiled and took an ample bite.

"I'd really like a beer with this," Summer grinned and dug in as well. After a few minutes she asked, "What time is the appointment with Turney?"

"You don't miss a thing, do you?" Kit grimaced playfully, knowing she hadn't told her friend that she already made an appointment. "It's at 1:00. We have about 15 minutes before she's expecting us."

"Us?"

"Of course, 'us'! You want to know what's going on, don't you?"

"Yes. I'm glad that you are including me in this."

The office was not easy to find as it was on that side alley off the main street. The door was flat against the brick wall with only the street address number painted on its window.

The women stepped in and had to allow their eyes to adjust as it was dimly lit. The hallway led to four more doors, and the elevator. Since the office was three flights up, they opted to take the elevator. When the door opened, straight ahead of them a door had "Turney Investigations" printed in script writing. Taking a moment to decide whether or not she should knock on the door, Kit finally just opened it.

A small waiting room without a window had two chairs with an end table and lamp between them on the left. A few women's magazines were on a low table to the right along with a fancy coat rack.

The door at the end of the room opened and a tall, thin woman of about 60 said, "Hello! Louise Turney," as she held out her hand.

Kit walked forward and shook her hand. "Kathryn Anderson. And this is my friend Summer Moon."

Louise shook Summer's hand as well and said, "Please call me Lou. Come in and relax."

Summer knew that "Louise" Turney had been born "Louis." Much to her credit, thought Summer, Kit made no judgments about Lou. When they walked into the inner office there was no mistaking the feminine touch however. Almost the entire back wall was a window that looked over Pittford. What appeared to have once been a low seat stretched in front of the window and was filled with plants, pictures, and memorabilia. A desk to the one side had framed certificates behind it and several file cabinets to the side. The flatscreen monitor had a colorful screensaver bouncing about on it, and there was the preverbal pile of papers showing that a lot of work was being done.

Lou led them to the other side of the large room, however and motioned for them to be seated. A Victorian settee faced two large wing backed chairs, all in a rose damask upholstery. The oak coffee table between them held a tray of glasses, assorted sodas, tea, water, and an ice bucket.

"I have been most interested in what we talked about yesterday, Kathryn," Lou began as she put some ice in a glass. "Have you decided to go ahead with an investigation?"

"Yes," Kit began and looked at Summer who shook her head 'yes' as well. "I thought you were a secretary when I talked with you."

"Well, I am ... and the owner as well." Lou held a glass with ice up and smiled. Summer, understanding said,

"Water please." She took the glass and the bottle of water from Lou and poured it for herself.

Another glass with ice was offered to Kit. "Tea please," and Lou handed her a bottled tea.

She made herself an iced tea, took a long drink, and put it down and picked up a clipboard from the settee. "Well, then, let's get started."

The women talked for the next hour about the book that Bill had kept and Kit showed Lou the newspaper clippings. She and Summer expressed all of their suspicions, all the happenings Kit thought to be threats, and all the questions raised by things other people said. Bill's not having his lucky fishing hat with him seemed to impress Lou as much as it had Tyler. Experienced fishermen just didn't leave their hats, and the flies they create, at home if they intended on fishing.

They spoke of the bracero boss and what they had seen at the flea market. Kit also mentioned David Melton's death last year and how the Mexican snow shoveller having discovered Melton and then was whisked away to Mexico. Could he have killed Melton or just covered up for the murderer?

"And it was very odd the teenager was so interested in what I was doing looking up Melton's death at the library."

By the time the women left, they both felt assured that Lou was going to be able to get to a resolution concerning the matter. All they had to do to help now was to not talk with her if and when she came to Kensington. Lou liked to keep a low profile.

On their way home Kit said, "That was certainly unusual."

"How so?"

"I've never known …" Kit began.

"Lou is remarkable."

"I was going to say I've never known anyone with such attentiveness to detail. That is what is unusual. I was impressed to see how thorough she is," Kit answered.

Summer sighed. "Mea Culpa. I'm just sensitive to people putting her down because of her life choices."

"Ah, you have known Lou for a while."

"Yes. I met her the first week I moved here. She was very helpful in my relocation and establishment of my shop."

"I hope one day you will know me as well," Kit answered, "to understand I am not prejudiced." She was hurt that Summer thought so little of her.

Summer took one hand off the wheel and put it on top of Kit's hand. "I should have known better. Forgive me?"

"I swear, you do know what people are thinking; of course all is well," Kit laughed.

By 6:50 that evening Kit had finished folding what little laundry she had and was ready for her date with Tyler. The phone rang but she opted to not answer it. If it were Tyler, he would call back. If it were not, she didn't want to bother with any nonsense that night.

Tyler was at her door by 7:00. He wore a light green sports jacket over an open collared white shirt and dark green pants. He didn't want to be too casual and yet he was tired of wearing uniforms every day.

Kit welcomed him into her kitchen with a warm hug. "It's nice to see what a prompt person you are!"

"I've been sitting outside in the alley for a while just so I didn't appear too eager," he laughed.

"Did you just call me?" she asked offhandedly.

"Me? No. Why? Didn't you answer it?"

"I just didn't want to have anything spoil this evening," she remarked as she picked up her handbag.

Tyler pulled her into his arms again. "Darling, nothing can ruin what we have together. This is just one night of a whole lifetime ahead of us."

Kit melted closer to him and thought she certainly hoped so.

She had opted for a soft pink chiffon outfit that set off her raven hair and wore her 3" heels just because Tyler was so much taller than she.

"You look stunning," Tyler smiled as he opened the door for her.

"Thank you, kind sir. It may take a while to navigate these stairs in these shoes."

Sexy shoes, thought Tyler. Kathryn was such a beautiful woman, and he thought himself very fortunate that she was in love with him. He took her elbow and helped her down the stairs and into the LeBaron.

Kit smiled as he got into the sedan. "What is that song you're whistling?"

Tyler stopped, looked at Kit and started laughing. "I wasn't aware that I was."

"Happy, or planning mayhem?" Kit asked with a slight grin and raised eyebrows.

"You betcha'" he grinned back and pulled out of the alley.

The countryside looked green and lush where the farms had irrigation. The corn will most likely reach "knee high by the fourth of July" in those fields," Kit commented.

Tyler nodded his head in agreement. "The drought conditions are problematic in the fields that are not being irrigated."

"Is there still time to come out of this if it rains?"

"Possibly." Tyler turned into a lookout place off the main highway. "Have you seen Emerald Lake from up here?"

"Not recently," Kit giggled.

Tyler stopped the car and then went to open Kit's door. "Let's take a walk."

Kit thought of her heels and wondered how wise it was to be doing so; and then, in an instant, she wondered if Tyler was going to push her over the side. He took her arm and maneuvered her over to the railing. Her heart was racing but she tried to not panic.

The sight below was breathtaking; and for a moment, she forgot her fear. Fireflies still danced overhead and the setting sun was sending streaks of red across the lake.

"There's the inn," Tyler pointed to a brightly-lit building with strings of lights all the way to the water's edge. Several boats were moored there and some had multi-colored strings of lights as well. He pulled a towel out from under his jacket and put it on the ground in front of her.

Kneeling down on one knee he said, "Kathryn, I have loved you for a long time. I just wasn't sure that you'd have an old rascal like me. Will you marry me?"

Kit began to cry softly. "You're not old, Tyler – but you are a rascal. Of course I will marry you."

He stood up and fished around under his jacket again and pulled out a ring box. "I got this when I was at the capital last week. I hope you like it."

The diamond was surrounded by smaller blue topaz gemstones, the same color as Kit's eyes. "It's beautiful," was all she could say. How could she even think that Tyler was behind all these deaths?

He slipped the ring on her finger and Kit said, "It fits perfectly."

Tyler was pleased with himself. "The forensic work I do gives me a good eye for things like that."

Kit leaned toward him. "You were pretty confident I'd say 'yes,'" she smiled as he nodded. They kissed softly, tenderly. How would she ever live if she lost him now.

"Would you like to stay longer, my love?" Tyler interrupted her thoughts as he picked up the towel.

"You thought of everything," Kit laughed softly about the towel. "We should probably go."

"Well, the reservations are for 7:30." Tyler helped her back into the car and soon they were driving toward the Inn.

Kit moved her hand to catch the car lights that came through the sedan's windows from time to time just to see the stones sparkle. When they got to the Inn, she was sure that everyone there was watching them. She felt the center of attention.

Indeed, many heads turned to see the sheriff and a lady friend out on the town. Their progress to their table was interrupted more than a few times with officials from both Kensington and surrounding towns hailing Tyler. Kit saw Lou Turney at a table across the room but was careful to not be too obvious in her recognition.

"Well, we are 'out', my dear," Tyler grinned at her.

"Are you okay with that?"

"Absolutely. I want everyone to know you are the future Mrs. Stone."

"Oh," Kit caught her breath. "I didn't even think of that. I've been used to being 'Mrs. Anderson' at school and everyone calls me 'Bates' here. This is going to take a while to get used to."

The waiter appeared with a wine list and some "specials" suggestions. The braised beef tips with portabella mushrooms and Asiago cheesestuffed pasta caught Kit's ear, and both she and Tyler ordered that special.

"Two weeks from now is the Fourth," Tyler began, "and as much as I want to spend it with you, I am going to have to be on duty, as well as the deputies, and some special people we hire. I just want you to know that usually my holidays are like that."

"I do understand, Ty. It's the nature of your business."

"After things settle down again in town, we probably should talk about what you'd like to do."

"Meaning?"

"The Book Store, or finding work as a teacher near by, or not working at all."

"It's all a whirlwind, Ty. I came to town for Bill's funeral and suddenly I was a book store owner. I just couldn't get around to making class room plans for this fall. Perhaps my staying here was not just to find Bill's killer. It was to find myself."

"And did you?"

"If admitting that I was still in love with you counts, then yes."

They were interrupted with the waiter bringing their meal. The first bite was heavenly. "This is excellent," Kit said.

"You're right. The chef here is well known for her innovative dinners.

"About the Fourth," Kit began, "Summer and I will get along just fine. I do understand your responsibilities, Tyler."

"I'm glad you and Summer have become such good friends," Tyler said. He went back to the discussion of the Fourth. "The VFW is having a hog roast after the parade. Maybe we could meet there for lunch."

"And the fireworks?"

"After the fireworks we can have our own." Tyler grinned as he watched Kit watching how her ring sparkled.

INVESTIGATIONS – Chapter Five

Tyler spent the night at Kit's place and left about 5:00 a.m. the next morning. "I'm on duty tonight," Tyler said. "Can we get together on Sunday?"

"Absolutely," Kit purred at him and wrapped her arms around his waist.

"Remember I love you," Tyler said. He kissed her on her forehead and Kit nodded her head.

"Be careful. I love you too."

After Kit saw him off she went back to the warm bed they had just shared. She drifted back to sleep. A few hours later Kit woke up on her stomach, hugging her pillow, remembering Tyler's caresses, his kisses, and how alive she felt in his arms. She rolled over, stretched, and put her hand up so that the morning light hit her engagement ring. Watching how the stones seem to dance in the light had not lost its fascination for her. More so, she was beginning to believe that Tyler's love was real. Any misgivings she had about him were dissolving with each day that passed.

Kit began her day as usual, with stretching exercises in the kitchen. She set the tea water to boil. She popped in a CD and did knee lifts, using a chair for support. Next came toe touches and cross-the-body toe touches. She really wasn't trying, but had lost about eight pounds since coming to Kensington. Knowing that it would be easy to regain those few pounds, she was careful to not indulge in her passion for late night ice cream. In fact, she had not had the treat for the past three weeks. Although she was often hungry, she was just too busy to indulge.

The tea kettle's whistle signaled the end of her workout. Hmmmm, she mused to herself, that wasn't really working very hard. She poured the heated water over the tea leaves and covered the cup with the saucer. Kit had learned to steep the tea that way from her grandmother. She smiled as she allowed her mind to wander back to her teen years and how Gran had given her something, like this simple way of steeping tea, to perpetuate their family customs. She would have liked Tyler.

After taking her cup of tea into the bathroom, she started the shower and took a good look at herself in the full length mirror before stepping into the tub. Kit was easily 35 pounds overweight but ceased feeling self conscious after her times at Sun Harbor. Summer had talked with her about self-acceptance and it had given Kit a sense of freedom to be who she was at the moment. And Tyler accepts me as well – just the way I am, she thought. Still, Kit's fantasy was to be fit. She knew many things worked together for a healthy mind, body, and spirit. Getting her life together was a great start.

The hot water felt especially comforting this morning. She dressed casually, and fixed a bowl of oatmeal with cinnamon and raisins. She finished her tea, now cold, swirled the dregs about and flipped the cup into her saucer. Her Gran also gifted her with the knowledge of reading tea leaves.

The area in the cup devoted to the past held leaves all piled upon one another. Yes. That's the way the past has been – messed up. The present day area showed a few butterflies and birds and a leaf symbolic of marriage – a diamond shape. Creatures of the air – were always light and promising. Of course the diamond hit the nail on the head. Ah, thought Kit, let's see what the future holds. She turned the cup around and around to make sure she was seeing everything. The cross would ordinarily mean hope but today the leaves stuck to each other so the cross shape was more like an elongated "x". Despair or death, Kit said aloud. She shook her head, rinsed out the cup and went downstairs to work.

Kit worked in the book store for a couple of hours. She answered the phone, taking one order and making up information about a sale on the Fourth.

With only one more week to prepare for the Fourth, she did the ever-necessary dusting, prepared an inventory for the sidewalk sale, and then went over the morning mail. It was difficult for her to concentrate, however, as she wanted to tell Summer about being engaged. So, she stacked the mail orders to one side and decided to fill them after she talked with her friend.

Kit put the "Back in 15 Minutes" sign up on the front door and locked the shop. She walked the short distance to the Mystic Spinner noting how warm it had become so early in the day. The streets were already filled with activity as the town was beginning to fill with holiday vacationers and she knew her shop would be busy later on as well.

The wind chimes sounded as she went into the new age shop, and today the aroma of patchouli filled the air. Summer was showing some crystals to a customer so Kit looked around in the divination section until the sale was made. Kit had always admired the alabaster runes and made a mental note to purchase a set. She remembered there was a book on the Celtic stones in her own shop and made another mental note to read the book, if there was ever time, she mused.

"Greetings, Kit, what brings you out so early?" Summer asked as the customer left.

"Oh, I don't know," Kit said slowly and walked over to the counter. "I just thought I'd show you," she paused, and thrust her hand toward Summer, "this!"

Summer's mouth dropped open as she took Kit's hand and looked at the engagement ring. She didn't say anything but came around the corner and took Kit into her arms. "Bill would have been so pleased. Oh, Kit, this is wonderful."

Kit laughed. "I think so too."

Summer stood back and looked at her friend. "I hope all of your fears about Tyler are gone."

"Ninety-nine percent," Kit responded. "The man I know just couldn't be involved in those murders."

"Well, that's better than last week," Summer said. She wiped her eyes, and went back behind the counter to finish up her last sale's paperwork.

"Are you going to set up for the sidewalk sale on the Fourth?" Kit asked.

"Yes. How about you?"

"Definitely. The parade goes right by our shops."

"Yes, it's a good opportunity."

"How would you like to go to the hog roast after the parade? I'm supposed to meet Tyler there. It would be so much fun!"

"Well, I hate to be a tag-a-long, Kit."

"Don't you ever say that, Summer. You would have been my ... well, you have become like a sister to me."

Summer bit her lip and had to wipe her eyes again. "I swear, Kit, you're going to make me lose it yet!"

Kit reached over the counter and took Summer's hand. "Listen here, you're entitled to cry as much as you like. And I can't imagine me making you do anything!"

Summer smiled and nodded her head. "Thank you. Of course you're right."

"Tyler's going to be involved with the fire works that night. Would you care to watch them with me?" Kit smiled.

"It's a date! You can see them from the knoll overlooking the lake. We can take my Jeep."

"Great! We can coordinate times later," Kit nodded and left the shop. She glanced back through the shop's windows as she walked toward the book store and saw Summer holding a tissue to her eyes.

She was strong, this woman from California. To the general public, she had it all together. Summer had lost her husband last year and then Bill. Suddenly Kit realized how much they had in common.

She had lost her husband, Gregg last year and now ... no, she would not live in fear of losing Tyler. It just could not be so.

The phone was ringing as Kit unlocked the door. She just answered it in time. It was the car dealer asking her to come see the renovated Jeep. She told him she would be there in a few minutes.

Kit watched as one of the mechanics drove the Jeep into the front parking lot of the dealership. It looked great. It sounded strong. She smiled at the salesman. "So, what do you think?" he asked.

"Let's talk warranty and price," Kit said.

After about a half-hour all the papers were signed. The down payment check was signed and Kit decided she had made a great deal.

"You know, I'm just making $100 over my costs, young lady."

"Thank you for being so understanding. By the way, did you fill up the tank?"

The salesman chuckled and shook his head. "There goes my profit."

Kit sat quietly with a pleasant smile.

"Okay. Take her out to the side of the shop. I'll meet you there at the gas pump."

"Thank you." Kit smiled and shook his hand. She was pretty smug about her purchase.

Kit parked her jeep in the back alley. She would tell Summer and Tyler later. She decided to clean and sort for the Fourth of July sale, so she took her ring off to make sure she didn't mar it and put it in the cash box. She started a box with items she intended to put into the sidewalk sale. There were extra copies of some best sellers that had been marked as overstocked. Under appreciated, she thought. She wondered if Bill read everything that he sold and then she decided he would never have had time.

Kit found the Celtic Runes book and leafed through it for a few minutes. Then, she took it to the front counter with the intention of reading it later.

There were cute book markers and some reading lights that had not sold. She could probably cut the price on them. Maybe she would have a drawing for a free book, and she went about designing tickets that could be filled out by customers. Later she was on her knees washing some lower book shelves, deep in marketing ideas when the bells on the door rang. Kit thought her first customer for the day had arrived. She wiped her hands on a towel and stood up.

"Hello, Kitty!" Tom's pleasant voice boomed!

"Tom, so glad to see you!" Kit began. She wanted to know about what he had learned in the ongoing investigation and wanted to tell him about her and Tyler.

"Same here," he smiled

"I have so much to talk with you about. Let's see, First, I'll ask you a strange question. In all of your travels around the area, have you seen a dark sedan that has its windows tinted? It's not a Michigan car."

"Why do you ask something like that?" Tom grinned uneasily.

"Well, Summer and I were in Pittford and saw two young men being arrested by the police. As we drove by this sedan seemed to be just sitting there watching. When the police put the handcuffs on the men, the car drove away slowly."

"And that seemed suspicious to you?"

"Yes."

"And what did Summer think?"

"Well, she suggested that I write the license number down. Here," she started and went behind the counter and dug into her purse. "This is the number," she finished and handed him the slip of paper. "I forgot about giving it to Tyler. Will you give it to him? I think his dope investigation team should have it."

Tom took the paper. "New Mexico. Okay, I'll deliver it. What took you to Pittford?"

"I've hired Lou Turney."

"Him? The investigator?" Tom rolled his eyes skyward.

"Yes, her," she attempted to correct Tom and realized it fell on deaf ears. "I didn't think we were making much progress," Kit said.

"Well, if you want to waste your money, go ahead," Tom responded, visibly annoyed, and then changed the subject. "I'm here for a few days and wanted to know if you'd like to lie out on a blanket, under the stars, and watch the fireworks the Fourth?"

At first Kit didn't know what to say. "Well, I already have plans with Summer. I guess you could come with us."

"Don't trouble yourself. I told you Summer Moon is dangerous. She's got you chasing strange cars now. If you don't want to listen to me, that's your problem," Tom answered angrily. "There's more than one woman in this town that would be happy to go with me."

"Tom, I ..." Kit began, but Tom left abruptly. She didn't have time to ask him if he had learned anything more about Bill's death, nor did she tell him of her engagement to his brother.

Tom went over to "Monique's" even though it was not open yet. Monica opened the office door for him. He would make Kit jealous once she saw him with this sexy lady.

"You look upset, Tom," Monica observed.

"Well, it's two-fold, my dear."

"Come in and have something cold to drink." Monica led the way into the restaurant kitchen and fixed two tall Arnold Palmers.

"Thanks," Tom smiled and took a long drink. "That's better."

"Ah, Monique always has an answer," Monica cooed with a French accent.

"First, my friend Kitty is flirting with a big hurt; seems she's involved with that red haired witch, Summer Moon."

"Yes, I saw them here together, but you can not do anything about that."

"True. I'm hoping you can help me with the second problem however."

"Anything," Monica said and meant it fully.

"Would you share a bottle of wine with me and watch the fireworks under the stars the Fourth?"

Monica's heart pounded but she answered coolly, "that would be delightful, Tom. Perhaps you'd like to go to the hog roast after the parade?"

"Sounds good. I'll pick you up around noon." He downed the drink, reached over, pecked her on the cheek, and left her standing in the kitchen.

Monica was pleased that he had finally come to his senses and recognized what an exquisite creature she was. She was totally unaware of Tom's using her.

Kit's sales had been good since she re-opened the store and she found herself thinking of talking to Summer about planning additions to the building. Since Summer had said she would like to be a partner and because Kit was going to be married, there was no reason to sell the business now. She dialed her real estate agent.

"Hello, Sharon," Kit said when the agent answered the phone. "I've decided not to list the book store after all."

"I see. Well, once someone gets used to this small town living, it's unlikely they want to leave," the agent replied. "If you change your mind, you know where to find me!"

"Thanks. Have a great weekend!"

"You too, Kathryn!"

There, that was accomplished. The rest of the morning flew by rapidly, waiting on customers, cleaning, and sorting for the sale. She happened to notice the mysterious black sedan go by her store slowly when she was arranging best sellers in the front window. It was eerie not to be able to see inside the car.

At the same time Summer was walking toward the shop, Kit came to the door. Both women watched the sedan turn the corner and head for the lake. "That creeps me out," Kit commented.

"Do you get a feeling that we're being watched?" Summer asked.

"It wouldn't take much for me to believe that."

"Lunch?" Summer asked.

"Monique's or the Dive?"

"I opt for the Dive today. A chili dog sounds great."

Kit retrieved her engagement ring, took a moment to admire its sparkle and grabbed her purse.

Summer watched with amusement.

Kit put up the "back in one hour" sign and locked the door as they left.

The Dive's patio was behind a tall wooden fence. Customers ordered at the window and sat at one of the many picnic tables behind the fencing.

"Well, if it isn't the town's finest," Summer smiled at two deputies at one of the tables. They smiled broadly and tipped their hats as the women passed by.

"I don't recognize the deputy with Cal," Kit said.

"They're beefing up the force for the Fourth," Summer answered. "Tyler knows the town." They were distracted by loud, sharp barking on the other side of the fence. The women looked toward the gate as the deputies left their food at their table and walked toward the commotion.

The women ordered their chili dogs and were sitting at one of the picnic tables in the shade as Cal returned.

"Everything okay?" Summer ventured.

"Yeah," laughed Cal. "*Una tourista* had a problem." He gathered up the food from their table and started to leave.

"Where's the new deputy?" Kit asked as he passed their table.

"He's in the squad car with the kid we picked up. The kid's high and was bothering Mrs. Jewel's dog. We're takin' him in. Damn dopers."

Kit and Summer looked out to the street and then at each other. Simultaneously they said, "the black sedan."

"I gave the license plate number to Tom." Kit offered.

"He may or may not get it to Tyler," Summer said and bit into the chili dog.

"Why?" Kit asked and then took a long drink of iced tea.

Summer had to wipe her chin before answering. "Tom is just the kind that would try to take the glory away from Tyler."

"Glory?"

"You know, catch the 'bad guys'," Summer answered.

"I think I'm going to concentrate on this Reuben and tea and let the boys sort out whatever is going on," Kit shook her head.

Summer nodded in agreement, but decided she needed to do some sleuthing on her own, beginning with talking to Sun Harbor's caretaker again.

Kit closed the book store at the stroke of five. She wanted to get to the library before it closed at 6:00 p.m. She took her notebook with data about team members' deaths, and was seated in front of the library's microfiche reader by 5:15.

She started with state-wide newspapers and was pleased to know the library was so up-to-date with their films. Kit had already accessed Melton's death and gleaned more information from Melton's son. She decided to go back a few years and look up Matthew Spencer's obituary from July of 2008 because she thought it would contain more information that the notice Bill had kept. It didn't take her long to find the right time frame. Kit looked up to see the same teenaged girl coming into the library that had questioned her the past Monday while using the microfiche machine.

Kit ignored her. Probably a coincidence, she thought, until the girl walked directly behind her. Kit turned to her. "Did you ask the librarian about using these machines?"

Startled, the teenager just shook her head and moved on. Kit carefully moved the machine to the obituary section of each of the weekly papers. As she focused in on Spencer's death, the teenager reappeared, lingering behind her. Kit turned the light off so the records would not show.

"I really don't like your standing here." Kit stated.

"It's a free country."

"Do I have to call the librarian so I have some privacy?"

The girl swore under her breath, and left, but not before making sure she read the label on the microfiche envelope.

Kit decided she would mention something to the librarian but right now she needed to concentrate on getting information on Spencer's obituary.

"Matthew Spencer, 37, Pittsford, was the victim of a one-car accident late Friday evening. His car appeared to be forced off Old River Road north of town. It was the bridge leading to the dam on Maple Lake. The car plummeted down the steep embankment and wasn't found until the next morning. He leaves a wife, Brenda and two daughters, Anna and Sylvia, and his parents Alan and Wilma."

Kit selected the information, printed it and then looked up Pittsford's phone listings. She copied Brenda Spencer's phone number down and shut the machine off. Since it was not 6:00 p.m. yet she went to the librarian's office and knocked on the door.

"Hello. May I help you?" the librarian asked.

"Hello. I'm not sure if it's just me, or if I need to complain," Kit said.

The librarian visibly stiffened. "Go ahead."

"There is a teenaged girl that seems to be very interested in my use of the microfiche machine."

"Has she harmed you?"

"No. She just doesn't respect my privacy."

"Well, youngsters are inquisitive. That's how they learn."

Kit knew she was getting no where. "You're right. Thanks anyway."

Kit walked back to the bookstore thinking about how the librarian could have called the girl to spy on what Kit was doing. "Ridiculous!" Kit said aloud as she let herself in and then locked the door behind her. She went directly to the office and dialed Brenda Spencer.

"Good evening," Brenda answered.

"Good evening, Mrs. Spencer. This is Kathryn Bates Anderson. If you have time to talk, I'd like to ask you a few questions."

"About what?" Brenda asked.

"My brother, Bill Bates, drown the first of the month."

"Yes. I read about it."

"Well, it seems to be a connection with his death and with your husband Matthew's death."

Brenda was silent.

"I know it sounds far fetched," Kit said.

"You mean the fact that my husband Matt, and your brother Bill, were both murdered?"

Kit's heart beat quicker. "Yes. I believe that."

"I have not had closure on Matt's death because of that 'elusive' hit-and-run driver. It was intentional. I just know it. What can I do to help?"

"I have hired an investigator. May I give her your phone number? She will need permission to investigate your husband's accident as well."

"By all means. Keep me informed."

"You'll hear from Lou Tourney soon."

"Thank you. Good bye."

Summer called soon afterwards. "Hi. Would you like to go the lake tonight?"

"Hi yourself. I'd like to talk with you anyway. Sounds like a good idea. Tyler's on duty. And, oh, I have a surprise for you."

"What's that?"

"I got a Jeep so, I'll drive."

"Super."

"I'll pick you up in a half-hour."

"See you."

"Okay." Kit dialed the sheriff's office and asked for Tyler.

"Tyler Stone," Tyler said.

"Hi, Tyler. I'm going out to the lake with Summer tonight."

"Lucky gals. Be careful."

"We've both said that earlier today. You be careful too, my darling."

Tyler laughed. "I like being called 'darling'."

"Good. Talk with you tomorrow." Kit smiled.

"Bye."

Kit picked Summer up at her shop.

"Hey – good choice in wheels!" Summer smiled.

"You ought to know. I really liked your Jeep and thought this was a good car for this area. I've got so much to tell you."

"Kit. Will you do something for me, just because I ask?"

"What?"

"We both need to relax. Can we talk after dinner? It will help both of us."

"Hmmmm. Talk about a lesson in curbing my enthusiasm." Kit rolled her eyes. "Okay, sure."

"Thanks."

Summer and Kit were at Sun Harbor before sunset. The women spoke to some of the regular campers about the weather and ate dinner with Elly and Gus.

Finally, they were back at Summer's mobile home and Summer poured each of them a little wine. They sat out on her deck and watched the fireflies darting about. The music from the clubhouse echoed across the water. "Okay, I'm relaxed. Thank you for waiting. What have you learned?" Summer asked.

"What do you know about the town librarian?"

"She's business-like, unfriendly, and I don't trust her," answered Summer.

"You know how we've spoken about the teenagers being involved in mischief and so forth?"

Summer nodded yes.

"Well, I told you how that girl was very curious about my using the microfiche when I looked up Melton's obituary."

Summer nodded again.

"The girl was there again this afternoon when I looked up Matthew Spencer's obituary. Something inside of me is thinking the librarian would have had to call her, letting her know I was there."

"I'm not surprised. The sedan is often parked near the library."

"The sedan is often parked near Monique's as well," Kit said slowly.

"The plot thickens." Summer shook her head.

"There's more. I talked with Brenda Spencer."

"She talked with you?"

"Are you surprised?"

"Bill told me she was hospitalized after her husband's death."

"That's too bad. Well, she is convinced her husband's death was intentional."

"The hit-and-run driver," said Summer.

"Another dead-end. I'll call Lou Tourney when we get back to town."

In the morning Summer was nearing the back of the clubhouse. She intended to sit in the hot tub for a while. Geoff, the park caretaker drove up to the back door as she got there. "Good morning, Geoff," Summer said.

"Mornin' ma'am," he answered.

"Since there is no one else around, may I ask you a question?"

"I guess so; doesn't mean I can answer it."

"Thanks. It's about the night Bill drowned."

Geoff just stared at her.

"I know you said you didn't have a license, so you weren't supposed to be fishing. If your testimony is needed, saying you heard something splash into the water off the patrol boat, could you say you were just out for a quiet ride?"

"What are you getting at?"

"It may be important. I think Bill was murdered."

"Okay. I could say that during my *quiet ride* I saw a body being dumped into the lake."

"You saw it? I thought you had just heard it."

"Well, if I'm fishing, I didn't hear or see anything because I wasn't out there. But taking a quiet ride, I can tell you, and I'll tell the judge I saw a body being dumped into the lake – from the sheriff's patrol boat."

"Thank you, Geoff. As long as that is the truth it is fine."

"The quiet ride isn't the truth."

"A fine for fishing is far less than testifying about seeing a body being dumped, isn't it?"

"I ain't got money for a fine."

"I understand, Geoff. That can be taken care of – but it wouldn't be payment for testimony."

Geoff grunted, nodded his head, and walked toward the back door.

Summer felt as though another victory had been won.

The women decided to stay another night at the park. Tyler joined them for dinner, but had to go back into town. Kit told Tyler about the librarian, the teenager, and Spencer's death. She told him about talking to Brenda as well.

Summer kept the information from Geoff to herself. She didn't want him to come to any harm and knew he could always be asked for help later.

"That's a lot to find out by yourself. Be careful talking to a lot of people though. If someone is trying to run you out of town, the more people know that you are investigating, the more dangerous it is.

"I have another idea and that is to talk with Dan Gregory's widow."

"That just happened last week. It will probably be pretty raw for her."

"I know, but since Tom isn't coming up with anything, and your office is busy with other things, I have to keep going."

Monday morning Kit called Lou and the investigator came by the book store; and when no one was around, she kept her eyes on the books but said to Kit, "I've made a chart of water deaths and unknown circumstances, dates, and so forth. I've cross-referenced them, and now I'm going to start investigating the known dope peddlers to see if there was any connection. I'm also looking into the men involved with the championship team 20 years ago that are still alive."

"It sounds like you've made some progress."

Lou asked Kit, "Should I look anywhere else?"

The phone rang, interrupting their conversation. "Excuse me a moment," Kit said.

Music blared in the background, but no one answered. "Is anyone there?"

"There shouldn't be anyone *there* either!" an angry voice said.

Kit hung up the phone and turned to Lou. "Another threat."

"We may have to put a recorder on your phone."

"Maybe." Kit then told her about talking to Spencer's widow, gave Lou the widow's phone number, and about the librarian and the girl's curiosity. Kit was hesitant to say anything about Geoff and the patrol boat, so she did not.

When Lou left Kit chuckled. Lou really hadn't done anything more than what she had started herself.

Preparing for the sale the next few days Kit didn't have time to get back to the library. Summer had brought Dan Gregory's obituary from the newspaper and Kit kept it. She clipped it out and added it to her brother's yearbook records – but not before using a red pencil to write his jersey number on the back. She waited until Thursday afternoon, three weeks after Dan Gregory's death to call his widow in California.

"Hello, Mrs. Gregory," Kit said. "This is Kathryn Bates Anderson from Kensington, Michigan."

"Hello."

"I'm sorry for your loss."

"Who are you?"

"I'm Bill Bates' sister. Bill died at the beginning of the month."

"Did he know Dan?"

"Yes, they went to high school together."

"I don't know any of Dan's friends. We met at U.S.C."

"I'm sorry to have to ask you this," Kit said.

"Then don't. It's been hard enough without people calling."

"Once again, I'm sorry. It's just that I believe Bill was murdered."

"And what has this got to do with me?" She slammed the receiver down.

Kit felt depressed the rest of the day. She called Tyler to see if they could get together.

Tyler was still on duty but he came over to Kit's to have dinner with her. About half-way through their meal he was called away.

"Fine way to start July," he said.

"Busier, because of the holiday?"

"Yep. Lunch at the Dive tomorrow?" Tyler asked.

"Sure."

Tyler and Kit met for lunch the next day and Tyler told her what happened. They ate fried onion rings and burgers. "I had to leave last night because several young men had been arrested for possession and selling drugs."

"What's next?"

"Before the final decision about keeping them in Kensington or transporting them to Pittsford was made, they were bailed out of jail. "I suspect they are being ushered out of the state as we speak. We'll never see them in Michigan again."

"I have been seeing the mysterious black sedan in town a lot. Summer and I have been seeing that car around here and in Pittsford. Do you know about it, Tyler?"

"Yes. I've not been able to come up with anything concrete though."

"I gave the license number to Tom to give to you when we saw it in Pittsford."

"Really?" Tyler said disgusted. "I'll have to investigate that further"

Kit realized then that Summer was right. Tom had not given the plate number to Tyler.

Tyler's beeper went off.

"Gotta' go," he said while looking at the phone number. He looked into her eyes and said, "You know I love you, don't you?"

"Absolutely. Now go get those bad guys!" Kit grinned as Tyler left.

Kit went downstairs to the shop and found a message on the telephone answering machine. It was Lou.

"Kit, I'd like to meet with you and Summer. Can you come to Pittsford – Alamo Park at 2 this afternoon?"

Kit called Summer first and then called Lou to say they'd be there.

"Hi," Kit said when Summer answered again. "I'll drive to Pittsford."

"Great, I'll walk over."

Kit started down the back stairs to the alley where her jeep was parked The words "GO HOME" written on the sides of the vehicle were visible from the top of the steps. She ran down the stairs quickly and saw that all four tires were flat.

Summer walked through the back alley toward the bookstore and saw Kit just staring at her new vehicle.

"Oh good grief," Summer said. "I'll call the sheriff's office."

"Not now. We don't have time. Can you drive to Pittsford?"

"Sure. Let's go." The women walked in silence to the back of Summer's shop to get her Jeep.

"Kit, have you been physically threatened?"

"No, Summer, just my Jeep," Kit frowned and then giggled.

"Glad you have a sense of humor here."

"Got to laugh so I won't freak out," Kit responded.

Lou met them in Alamo Park. "I wanted you to know what is happening. I've been helping the state task force with the dope ring. I've learned the leaders get people to do their bidding – and take them out of the picture if they do not. Some young migrants have come up missing, but local authorities can't do anything about it – usually they don't have green cards so their families don't report them. The organization gets teenagers to do their dirty work."

"Just as Tyler thought," Kit told her. "My Jeep was vandalized today. Do you think that, and the calls I've been receiving could be from them?"

"Could very well be. I have theorized that Bill did not go along with being a 'dump site' for the dope. It would have been a good cover – people coming and going all the time."

Summer said, "Bill never mentioned it, and I think he would have."

"I think that he didn't want to involve you," Lou answered. "I've been checking into the black sedan you've been seeing. It's registered to a New Mexico businessman. The businessman is a regular at Monica's. I wouldn't doubt if she's involved some how."

Kit became upset. "This might be more of a problem than we suspected, but, did that mean all of those men on Bill's basketball team were involved?"

Lou answered, "No, it just seems to be similar circumstances."

"Well, thank you. What's next?"

"I think you should leave it up to the task force. If you two would be patient, it will all come out in a short while."

"Do you have a statement for me?"

Lou opened her briefcase. "If you ever need anything, just call." She handed the bill to Kit.

Kit dug into her purse for the check she had made out to Lou. She glanced at the bill and filled in the amount. "Thanks again."

"What do you think of that?" Kit asked Summer as they headed back to Kensington.

"If I were a betting person, I'd bet our Miss Lou has been mislead."

"This isn't over yet," Kit answered.

The Fourth of July was sunny and hot by 11 a.m. The parade started at the high school and wound through town and ended at the Veteran of Foreign Wars' Hall. It had been a Kensington tradition since Kit could remember.

Kit set up a table against her storefront, under the roof overhang so that she was shaded from the bright sun. A canon at the VFW hall sounded loudly, announcing the beginning of the parade.

Two police vehicles were in the lead. Tyler was driving the Kensington squad car and shared the road with a state police SUV, driven by a trooper.

Tyler smiled and waved as he drove by and then gave Kit a few short siren blasts. It gave her goose bumps to see him in this official capacity.

Next, the VFW color guard came by. Watching men of various ages carrying the flags, dressed in uniforms representing different service branches gave her goose bumps again. An open-topped convertible followed with three veterans from the Korean War that lived in the area. Her grandfather had fought in that war, Kit remembered. He would become very animated as he talked about it being called "a police action." Time goes by so quickly, she began to think and then decided to not go there today.

A huge bell, representing the liberty bell, was mounted on a small wagon and was being pulled by a garden tractor all decked out with American flags. It could be heard for blocks away, being rung by Tony, one of the local veterans of the Korean War, dressed like Uncle Sam. His tall, lanky frame and his natural flowing white hair made him look the part. She smiled and waved to him and he tipped his hat in return as he had each year she watched the parade.

The high school band played "I'm a Yankee Doodle Dandy" and did a high stepping strut. Both the girl and boy scouts marched proudly by, following by a mixture of both out-of-breath and physically fit parents and leaders.

People were milling about as the parade passed, stopping from time to time to watch a particular entry. Children scurried after candy that was thrown to them from the fire engines, fancy souped-up cars, historic vehicles, and floats. "Miss Kensington" smiled and waved from the back of a convertible advertising a local insurance agency.

The Keystone Cops were a hit, especially on such a hot day as this. They were riding a bicycle-built-for-two and showering people with their water guns.

Kit's sales went over well and she had quite a few entries in her drawing for a free book. The kids on decorated bikes were almost last, the horses following, and the area antique car and tractor buffs bringing up the rear of the parade.

The crowd had meandered down toward the VFW grounds so Kit stacked her sale items inside the door and was locking up when Summer arrived.

"All ready to 'pig out' at the hog roast?" she smiled.

"Tell me you didn't say that," Kit winced and then laughed.

When they arrived at the edge of the festivities they saw Tom with Monica.

Summer addressed Monica, "Who's minding the café?"

"Oh the luncheon service is closed due to hog roast," Monica answered as she and Tom moved close by.

"Wonder what wine Tom will suggest goes well with roast hog?" Summer whispered to Kit.

Kit smiled and then spotted Tyler. "There he is!" She waved to him.

Tyler strode over to them and kissed Kit on the cheek. "Hello, Love."

"You look so," and Kit paused, "official!" The threesome laughed.

"I'm so glad you two are 'official', Tyler. You two are made for each other!" Summer bubbled.

Tom had been standing close by, straining to hear what was being said. His mouth dropped open and then he turned to Monica. "Did you hear that?" he seethed.

"It appears your brother is about to be married."

"Kit will never marry him. I'll make sure to set her straight – prove that he's the murderer of all those men!"

Monica was confused, but didn't want Tom to know that. She just took his arm as they walked away.

The roasted hog was tender and the salads were plentiful. After eating together, Tyler had to excuse himself.

"Well, we can either stay here or open our sales again," Summer offered.

"Oh, I'd rather go back to the store," Kit replied.

They walked arm in arm back toward their shops on the main street, leaving the din of the crowd behind them. The school band started playing, and it helped the women to be in good spirits.

Summer picked Kit up at 9:30 that night and the two women watched the fireworks from Summer's jeep on a hill just outside of town. Most everyone from town was there also – just overlooking the lake. Kit knew Tyler out there but couldn't distinguish him from any of the other men with orange vests. Summer dropped Kit back to her shop by 11 p.m.

Tom and Monica watched most of the fireworks and he drove her back to her place. "More wine?" Monica asked, knowing the only way she would get him into bed was if he were plied with an expensive Merlot.

Tom took her roughly, not caring about her. He figured that they had enough to drink that she wouldn't know it anyway. He finished the bottle after Monica fell asleep and he drove to Kit's.

Tom stumbled up the back steps to the apartment. He would show Kit what a man he really was.

Kit, thinking it was Tyler, opened the door without looking. "Tom, what are you doing here?"

"Hey little Kitty, let me in," he grinned a lopsided grin at her.

"I think you'd better go home and sober up," Kit smiled but Tom started forcing the door open.

"Tom!" she reprimanded,

It made him angry. "Well, we don't have to do this peacefully," he growled at her as he pushed his way into the kitchen.

Kit knew he was stronger than she, even if he was drunk. Suddenly she was afraid of being raped. How could she stop him?

"Is there a problem?" Tyler's deep voice came from the top of the stairs.

"No problem, big brother," Tom reeled around. "Kit was just trying to make me leave. We had some great sex. How do you like 'seconds'?"

Tyler grabbed him by the collar and almost threw him down the stairs. "I have to drive him home. I'll be back as soon as I can, Kit."

Kit locked the door and realized she was still trembling. The phone ringing made her jump. It was another voiceless call.

Tyler threw Tom into the back of the squad car and drove off.

"You know how old you are, Tyler. Kit needs someone young and virile like me. I've got a great job and a wonderful future and she deserves someone who could provide with her that ... not just a sheriff's job." When Tyler didn't respond he added, "Don't you see how she looks at you with pity?"

Tyler kept his cool. He knew if he responded to his brother right now he would hurt him. When they arrived at the house they shared, he dragged Tom out and dumped him on the back step, not caring if Tom got inside or not.

Tyler knocked on Kit's door, and she made sure it was him before she opened it. He swept her up into his arms.

"Oh, Ty, you don't believe Tom, do you?" she asked and started to cry.

"Never, little kitten – as long as you believe in me." They stood there in the kitchen for a few minutes until Kit calmed down.

Tyler swept her up into his arms and carried her through the darkened apartment. They undressed and held each other without initiating anything other than sharing the warmth and comfort of their being together. Kit felt at peace for the first time in weeks.

In the morning, after making love, they showered together, laughing and talking like there were no dark secrets, no mysteries plaguing them, and nothing but their love surrounding them. When Tyler left, a depression descended on Kit. She wondered if last night was the beginning of their life together or their final hurrah.

Summer called and asked Kit to go to the lake with her, just to pick up some things at her home. Summer was feeling rather anxious for some unknown reason and just wanted the company.

"What's up?" Kit asked.

"Well, I wanted you to know I spoke to Geoff last weekend."

"And?"

"And he told me he saw Bill's body being dumped into the lake."

"Oh my God, Summer. There is no question at all now."

"That's right. We can't tell anyone unless this comes to trial, Kit."

"Why?"

"Geoff's life might be in danger."

"You're saying we can't even tell Tyler?"

"Not for a while. Are you okay with that?"

"Not happy, but okay," Kit answered.

As they drove back into Kensington, Summer noticed the mysterious sedan down one of the side roads. She recognized the person talking to the driver of the sedan but didn't say anything.

"Summer, you look like you've seen a ghost!"

Not wanting to alarm Kit, she lied, "No, Kit, I was just thinking about Bill."

"Yeah, it's hard sometimes," Kit answered.

Summer dropped Kit off at the book store, made sure she was inside okay and then hurried to her own place. She had an idea to follow up on and for the next half-hour searched through her letters and notebooks from Bill. She brewed some mint tea and took the stack into her living room. Finally, she found a poem Bill had written just after Mike Stone's death.

Summer had read through everything the first week after Bill's death, and this particular entry hadn't seemed significant until now. She read in Bill's own handwriting:

"And now another star has passed –
his glow once brightly burned
His fame is gone forevermore –
possessed through hard work earned
Taken away one fateful night –
an awful lesson learned
But now his life snuffed out, for what –
because a Stone was left unturned?"

    Bill had capitalized "Stone" – was he was talking about a person? Summer called Lou and told her she had some additional information. "No, I won't share it with you over the phone."
    Lou responded, "It just so happens that I'm going to Allenville this late afternoon and have to pass through Kensington about four. I'll stop at your place."
    "That will be fine," Summer responded and took the notebook to the library to copy the poem. She made one that came out rather light, so she tore it in half and threw it away. The second one came out darker, she paid for it and left.
    The same teenager that had watched Kit, saw that Summer had thrown something in the trash. When no one was looking, she retrieved the pieces of paper. Her boss would be very pleased.
    Lou got to the Mystic Spinner about 4:10 and was greeted by Summer. "I'm sure I know who killed Mike Stone and pretty sure Bill was killed because he knew also. Read this," Summer handed her the page.
    Lou had just started to read the poem when a Molotov cocktail sailed through the front window and burst, sending shards of glass in every direction. A jagged piece of window glass hit Lou on the side of her neck, and she collapsed immediately. An instant conflagration spread rapidly throughout the room. Summer was unhurt, but she tried picking the larger woman up. When that didn't work, she tried to drag her out; but by that time the flames were spreading and the shop with filling with smoke. A part of the

door frame came down just as Summer got to the front door opening and struck her in the head. She dropped right there motionless.

Shop owners in the vicinity had heard the explosion and ran out of their shops to investigate. People on the street were frozen in horror as they saw the growing fire inside the Mystic Spinner.

Kit also ran into the street to see what was going on. "Summer!" she screamed in horror when she saw the flames. She ran toward her friend's shop.

The librarian had been watching the shop to see what the bracero boss had cooked up to harass Summer. She was shocked to see the firebomb exploding, and called 911 immediately.

By the time Kit got to the scene she heard the sirens screaming toward them. The tobacconist caught Kit before she got to the Mystic Spinner's door, and she had to wrench herself away. He joined her then and they managed to pry open the door. Tyler's squad car came out of nowhere, tires squealing. He jumped out, leaving the lights and sirens going full blast and ran toward Kit. He told her to get back, and he and the tobacconist pulled Summer out into the street. Kit stumbled to her side, and Tyler handed her a handkerchief. "Press this very tightly over her wound," and he left them.

The ambulance arrived the same time as the fire department. Two paramedics immediately administered oxygen to Summer. She had not regained consciousness. Two others were standing by if needed. A deputy was shouting at a crowd of people to stand back

The water hoses were being attached to a nearby hydrant, while a firefighter looked inside. He charged in because he saw another person lying on the floor. He brought the lifeless woman out; the other paramedics sprang into action and took vital signs. One shook her head.

Tyler was talking with the fire chief as the volunteers hosed down anything smoldering in the small shop. The fire was out quickly but left books washed off the shelves unto the floor. The lovely crystals in the windows were broken, paintings were scorched. A few of the remaining wind chimes clanked sadly.

One of the paramedics stayed with Lou, and Tyler went to check her status. Lou had died, most likely from the loss of blood where the glass cut her carotid artery. Now this crime involved arson and murder.

Summer was being taken to the Kensington clinic by the paramedics, and Tyler came over to comfort Kit for a moment. He had to tell her about Lou.

"I want to go to the clinic with Summer," she said quickly. She was waiting to get into the ambulance.

Tyler pulled her close and said, "Yes, of course. You have to know that Lou is gone."

"Oh, my God, Tyler," Kit felt her knees start to buckle, but Tyler held her steady.

"Be careful, Kit. I have to stay here a while, and then I'll come to the clinic."

Kit was frantic with worry for her friend, and she was in shock about Lou. The paramedic driver helped Kit into the ambulance. The tobacconist called to her through the open door that he'd close up the book store for her, and she vaguely heard and thanked him. She held Summer's hand and prayed the whole way to the hospital.

It appeared that her friend suffered a severe head injury. Once seen at the clinic, it was determined that she should be transferred to the Pittsford Hospital and was being prepared to transfer when Tyler got to the clinic.

"Oh, Ty, she's hurt so badly," Kit worried openly now that Tyler was there. He gathered her in his arms and let her weep.

"We'll get to the bottom of this, Kit. Summer's a strong woman." He comforted her and tenderly massaged the top of her shoulders. "She'll be okay."

Kit took a deep breath. "You're right." She took a deep breath. "Is there anything left of the shop?"

"Sure," he answered. "The fire damage was not bad. It'll take time to clean up all the water damage though."

The nurse came out of Summer's area and told them she was being put into the ambulance for transfer.

As if reading her mind, Tyler said to Kit, "You can ride with me in the squad car. I'm sorry, though, you'll have to ride in the back seat; Department requirement."

"I don't mind, Tyler."

He radioed the office that he was going to the hospital and confirmed that his deputies were roping off the crime scene.

Crime scene, Kit thought. Yes, that's exactly what it was. Lou died there. Summer was fighting for her life.

Within an hour, Summer had been diagnosed with a closed head wound and was in an intensive care room, hooked to several monitors. Kit and Tyler stayed until the doctor in charge assured them they would be called if there were any changes. They made plans to return within a few hours anyway.

As they were leaving, the deputy, Carl, arrived. "Jim will be here in four hours," he told Tyler.

"Good," was Tyler's only response.

"What is that all about?" Kit asked as they left the hospital.

"Precaution."

"Do you think someone would really try to …" Kit said, her face ashen.

"Like I said, 'precaution'. It was a pre-meditated crime, Kit."

He moved a logbook, some pens, his gloves, and an extra walkie-talkie into the back seat so Kit could ride back to Kensington in the front with him.

"What about regulations?" Kit asked.

"Being broken," Tyler muttered. He helped her into the squad car.

He drove one-handed so that he could hold her hand with the other. "The only bad thing about seat belts," he grumbled. "I want to hold you."

"There's time later, I hope," she managed, her shoulders still shook uncontrollably.

Tyler received a call from the office when they were almost in Kensington. The fire marshal had arrived and wanted to talk with him.

"Do you want me to take you right home?"

"No, I'd like to hear what the fire marshal has to say. That is, if I may."

"Sure. We'll go to the crime scene."

'Crime scene' again, thought Kit.

The Mystic Spinner's entrance was cordoned off with the bright yellow "do not cross police lines" tape. Tyler spoke with the marshal as Kit peered in the windows. It was a mess, but only one area was scorched.

"Molotov cocktail," the marshal was saying.

"Thought so," Tyler responded and opened his arm for Kit to come close to him. "Hopefully someone on the street saw the vehicle."

Start with a dark-glassed sedan, thought Kit.

The marshal left and Kit and Tyler looked in the window again. "Can we get this boarded up tonight?" Kit asked.

"Sure." He flipped out his walkie-talkie and called the office. "Have Calvin board up the Spinner, Mary."

"Right-O, Sheriff," answered Mary.

He turned to Kit, "There, done. Do you want to go check your place?"

"Yes, and take a shower," she said.

Tyler smiled slightly, embarrassed that he hadn't noticed that Summer's blood was on Kit's clothes.

The book store had been locked up by the tobacconist and she made a mental note to thank him. Tyler came up stairs with Kit to make sure everything was alright. "I'd love to stay and sponge your back with lots of soapy bubbles." Tyler grinned. "But I need to get to the office." He wrapped her up in his arms. "I'll pick you up in an hour," he said and kissed the top of her head.

Kit smiled and nodded. She locked the door behind him, picked up a garbage bag from under the sink, and then quickly made her way to the bathroom. She stripped off her blood stained clothing and carefully dropped it into the garbage bag. Balancing herself against the sidewall of the shower, her head under the showerhead, she let the hot water flow directly on her for a long while.

Kit allowed herself to cry for a short time and then turned the temperature down on the water. By the time she was ready to come out, the water was cold and she felt very refreshed.

She brewed tea and drank it, wrapped only in her towel. While getting dressed, she checked the time and realized Tyler would be there shortly. The phone rang and thinking it was Tyler she pushed the button for the speaker phone. "Hello!"

There was no response and she quickly hit the 'record message' button as the caller growled, "Thought you'd like this."

A recording came on of the chaotic scene earlier. She heard the sirens and her own voice in the background talking to Summer as she cradled her. She heard Tyler offering her his handkerchief to hold on the wound. The voice came on again with a low rasping laugh and the phone went dead.

She switched off the recorder. It could have come from anyone who was there watching – even Tyler. She sat in a stupor for a few minutes.

Tyler's knock on the back door startled her. It took her a minute to let him in.

"Not ready yet?" he laughed.

"No."

Tyler could see she was in no mood for humor. "Are you okay, Kitty?"

"Yes," she lied. "Just distracted. I'll be ready in a few minutes."

Tyler had also showered and changed. He picked her up in his car so she was able to sit next to him and use the middle lap belt. He could sense that Kit's mood had changed again but decided to let her tell him what the problem was when she was ready to talk.

Kit wanted to tell Summer and Lou about the phone call and suddenly realized how impossible that was. She was totally alone. Why did the phone call make her distrust Tyler again?

SOLUTIONS – Chapter Six

Kit appreciated the quiet ride to the hospital. Hoping to feel the comfort she needed, she leaned against Tyler. He seemed to sense that she was still processing Bill's death; and now with the added stress of Summer's injuries, he felt that Kit was fragile. He didn't know the extent of what was going on in his fiancée's mind.

Tyler drove up to the front door. "I'll go park in the ramp and meet you at Summer's room."

Kit smiled, nodded and scooted out the door. She barely acknowledged the door man and crept slowly to the elevators with that odd feeling she always experienced when she went into hospitals. It probably stemmed from the conglomeration of chemical odors. She rode up to the fourth floor thinking the smell of death had to be disguised somehow. When did she become morbid?

The police officer was seated outside Summer's room. "Hello, Carl."

"Ma'am," he nodded his head.

From the doorway, Kit could see Summer hooked to a couple of monitors and an IV drip. She had to swallow hard not to cry as she hesitantly walked up to the bed. "Summer?"

Summer didn't respond at all. Her monitors just elevated a bit and Kit hoped that somehow her friend recognized her voice.

Kit stood next to the bed and took Summer's hand, speaking in slow, soft tones. The monitor didn't change. "Everything is under control, sweetie," Kit offered.

A nurse came in and checked the readouts on the monitor. "You keep talking to her. Maybe you'll help her wake up."

"Thanks. I brought a book of poetry along to read to her."

"Good idea. I'm sure the doctor would tell you that she's holding her own."

Kit nodded and sat down as the nurse left. She opened "The Rubiyat of Omar Khayyam" and began reading. Summer's monitor slowed again to near normal as Kit read.

In the background Kit was aware of Tyler talking to the officer outside the door.

Summer's monitor began to accelerate. Kit kept reading and watching the monitor at the same time.

Tyler came in. "Hello, ladies," he said cheerfully. Summer's monitor began to race and a warning light started to flash. Tyler frowned. "What's going on?"

"I'm not sure."

The nurse came in. "Will you both please step outside?" Kit was visibly shaken and Tyler took her arm as they left the room.

"Oh, Ty," Kit whimpered.

"She'll be okay. She's strong."

"Easy for you to say."

Tyler just held her and knew the words welled up from the emotional shock she just experienced. The nurse joined them. "I gave her an injection that the doctor had ordered if she needed some help sleeping. She's been through severe trauma."

"Yes," Kit answered and stepped away from Tyler. She approached Summer's door quietly and looked into the room.

Another officer arrived at that time to relieve Carl. Tyler talked with him, giving instructions that no one was to see the patient. Kit returned at that moment and stood quietly beside Tyler. He absentmindedly put his arm around her waist, and this time she did not recoil. She was just too tired and confused. Why had Tyler's voice upset Summer so much?

"Let me take you for some dinner. It's already past eight," Tyler offered as they walked to the parking ramp.

"All I want is some tea and toast."

"Okay, I'll take you home then."

"That would be fine. Maybe you'd like something also."

Tyler thought that what he needed right then wouldn't be on the menu that night. He'd not seen Kit this upset since the first day she came to Kensington after Bill drowned.

"Tea and toast for two?" The sheriff grinned.

Kit tried to reciprocate, but his attempt at humor was being lost in her confusion and fear.

Tyler waited until Kit had set the water to boil in the kettle to pull her into his arms. She immediately started to cry. "Go ahead, sweetie. Let it all out."

She wept so hard her shoulders trembled and Tyler sensed her crying was more than a simple reaction to Summer and Lou's disaster. She'll tell me in her own time, he thought. The kettle whistled and Kit managed to take a deep breath and stop crying.

She smiled up at Tyler. "Thanks, I needed that," and she turned to fix the tea.

Tyler spread strawberry preserves on a piece of toast as Kit used cream cheese and the preserves on hers.

"Are you feeling any better?" Tyler asked.

"Earl Grey's caffeine always does the trick." Kit took a slow sip.

"Are you going to tell me what's bothering you?"

He knows me well, thought Kit. "Actually, I got another phone call just before you picked me up."

"Why didn't you tell me?" Tyler said and put his tea down to listen carefully.

Kit got up and went to the phone. "Listen." She played back the growling message from the recorder. Tyler just stared at the phone and shook his head.

"It had to be from someone there."

"Someone close enough to hear us talking, Ty."

Was she was implying he was involved? "You can't believe?"

"Why did Summer's monitor go crazy when she heard your voice?"

"Kathryn?"

Kit slumped down into the chair next to him. She reached out and touched his arm. "Do you know how much I love you? I'm just so over my head in all of this. "

Tyler stood up, intending to leave. He was upset but thought better not to let her know. Still, she had not said that she did not suspect him.

"Will you hold me tonight?"

He smiled and his concerns dissolved when she asked him to stay. "Are you sure?"

"Of course."

Tyler gathered Kit into his arms, melting reservations of confusion and doubt. "Forgive me, Kit. Finding love and cultivating a relationship is new to me."

"With the turmoil surrounding us, it'll be a miracle to survive."

"I believe in miracles," Tyler whispered close to Kit's ear.

Kit made the first move to separate and led him into the bedroom. They sat on the edge of the bed silently embracing and soon they were laying together, their legs and arms entangled. They slept that way for hours.

Kit woke up about 3:00 a.m. to use the bathroom. Stumbling back toward the bed in the dark she noticed a strange glow outside. Carefully peeking through the blinds she spotted the dark sedan out on the street with its headlights on. Before she could wake Tyler, it drove on. Strange, she thought; like they're casing my place.

Kit eased in beside Tyler again and almost chuckled. Casing my place? When was this all going to end? She soon fell asleep again.

In the morning Tyler left before anyone was up in the neighborhood. "I have business at the capital today. I'll see you as soon as I can."

Kit held him tightly and thanked him for staying the night. They kissed and Tyler left. She prepared to spend some time at her shop and then at the hospital with Summer. The phone rang about 7:30 a.m.

"Hello, darling!" came her mother's lilting voice.

"Hi mom."

"I'm coming to Kensington to help out. I heard all about Summer's problem, not from you of course."

"Hmmm, you always have a way of making me feel guilty."

"Disguised as an offer of help," she laughed.

"Okay. I'm glad you'll be here."

"I'll meet you at your shop, say noonish?"

"Great. Drive carefully."

Kit felt better knowing that her mother would be around for moral support. She always loved Tyler anyway and could help Kit clear her mind.

At 10:30 Amanda arrived, early as usual. She busied herself dusting shelves as Kit waited on the few customers they had. Amanda also helped the junior high student, who won the July 4th drawing, pick out a book.

Kit and her mother went to the Dive for lunch. Kit told her everything from beginning to end. She hadn't even touched her lunch while Amanda ate, nodded, and just listened.

"Now, it's your turn, my dear." Amanda commanded, "Eat your lunch."

Kit ate her cold French fries and choked them down with her diet drink.

"Tyler is an honorable man. He has listened to everything you've said about your suspicions about Bill, about the drug ring, which is overwhelming. You have your reservations about Tom as well. He's been as helpful as he can, considering his line of work. You have a good support system. Let me simplify this all.

"Number one – Tyler is dealing with the murder of this woman you hired

"Number two – Added to that is his friend, Summer's injuries.

"Number three – He already has his hands full with some drug dealers

"Number four – Sometimes Tom is more help than the sheriff

"Number five – I know you care a great deal for Tom.

"Number six – You say you are in love with Tyler."

"And most importantly, number seven – listen to that still, peaceful voice God speaks to you with."

Kit started to comment but her mother quieted her. "You need to trust yourself, your own instincts before you can trust anyone else. You have put your trust in Tyler and in Tom to help you. God is faithful. Don't stop now."

"Good advice. Maybe I'm just thinking too hard. Do you want to go see Summer with me?"

"Of course."

"Let's go close up the shop."

Tom was waiting for them when they arrived.

"Amanda! What a vision you are!"

"Oh Tom, you always are one to say the right things!" she laughed.

"Hello, Kitty Cat." He smiled a toothy grin.

Kit unlocked the door and let them both in. "We were just going to see Summer."

"I see, well, I have news. I hired an investigator and he has found the man who killed your brother," Tom stated. "I told you it might rock this town, but as long as you were insistent and hired your own investigator, who unfortunately was killed ... well, grab your purse and we'll go meet him"

"What about Tyler? Shouldn't he know?"

"Oh, he knows. Why do you think he left town this morning? I doubt you'll see him again. Get your purse, let's go!"

"Mom?" Kit turned to Amanda.

"I'll close up the shop, and then go see Summer. Don't worry. Have faith."

Kit was heart sick, but she had to know what the evidence was against Tyler. Perhaps the investigator was wrong. Amanda watched Tom's Porsche speed out of town.

Only a few minutes passed before the door bell tinkled. It was Summer, being pushed in a wheel chair.

"Hello my dear!" Amanda greeted her with surprise.

"Hello, is Kit with you?"

"Well, that's a fine way to greet me."

"I'm sorry Amanda, but I have to talk to Kit.

"Can I help you? She's gone out of town for the afternoon."

Summer started shaking. "I have to tell her what I found. It's a poem written by Bill … and then, she has to know I saw Tom talking to the men in the black sedan. He must be involved in the drug dealings going on."

"What's that got to do with Kit?"

"Very quickly – the drug dealers coerce the migrant workers to do their bidding … like harassment, and most likely bombing the Spinner."

"And you saw Tom dealing with them?" Amanda's face paled.

"It's important that Kit knows. And I've got to talk to Tyler!"

"What's so important?" Tyler asked from the doorway. "Should you be out of the hospital?"

"Yes, I'm okay," Summer responded.

Amanda interrupted. "Tyler! Kit went with Tom to meet a private investigator."

"Oh no!" Summer cried. "I saw Tom talking to the men in the black sedan."

Tyler's face reddened. "I need to use the phone. Where's the phonebook?"

Amanda went behind the counter. She hurriedly pulled the directory from beneath a pile of books. A manila envelope fell to the floor and its contents spilled at Amanda's feet. She bent over to pick them up and saw the Polaroid snapshot of the dead cat.

Seeing her expression, Tyler asked. "What's the matter?"

Amanda handed the picture to him and he stared in disbelief. "Did Kit show this to you before?" he showed Summer. She shook her head.

Tyler said, "I guess I don't need to use the phone after all. This is enough proof to confirm what I learned – what I didn't want to believe."

Summer heard the pain in his voice before she saw his expression of grief. "What is it, Tyler?"

"Look at the reflection in the store window."

Summer gasped as she recognized Tom's silver Porsche in the picture.

"Do you have to drive so fast, Tom?" Kit asked nervously. The top was down and the wind was blowing sand into her eyes and whipping her hair onto her face as well.

He glanced at her from behind the silver coated sunglasses and then looked back to the road without answering.

"Tom?"

"I thought you like to live dangerously, Kitty Cat."

"Where did you get that idea?"

"Well, all those warnings, the calls, the notes, the dead cat. You still insisted on staying in town."

Kit shifted uneasily in the soft leather seat. She didn't remember telling him about the dead cat. Suddenly it dawned on her that the note had read, "You're next, Kitty Cat!" That was what Tom consistently called her.

Trying to calm her voice she said slowly, "Well, I'm glad you hired an investigator. Where are we going to meet him?"

Tom took the lake road and headed toward the more secluded area. It was anything but a smooth ride. His Porsche wasn't made for country driving. "He's at the old Simpson place."

"Why so secretive?"

"Why so many questions, sweetie?" he smiled and put his right arm about her shoulders.

"I just thought ..."

"Don't bother thinking. All of your questions will be answered shortly."

They roared up the driveway in a cloud of dust. Tom helped her from the car but held too tightly to her elbow as he led her up the porch steps. Maybe he expected her to run. He shoved her to the couch and then locked the front door. Pulling a gun from beneath his coat, he aimed it at Kit.

"It was you." Kit blanched. "Why?"

"I grew up feeling so sad for Uncle Mike. He was confined to that wheel chair because of that stupid accident when he was in the prime of his basketball career. He would have been some star player!" began Tom. "A couple of years ago Mike began to deteriorate and was in constant pain. That's when I decided to kill Matthew Spencer. He was the one driving the car, you know."

Kit casually looked to the windows trying to hide her fear. She knew the door had been locked.

"Pay attention, Kitty Cat!" Tom snapped at her. "Everything would have been okay. Spencer's death was considered an accident, but Uncle Mike suspected that I had been involved. He told me that I had to turn myself in ... that I needed special help. Me, need special help?" Tom waved his gun in the air. "It was Uncle Mike that needed constant help! He told me that if I didn't turn myself into the authorities he would. That's why I had to push him into our pool. I still can't believe how hard it was to force him over the edge. What a fighter."

Kit gasped and tears flowed unchecked.

"My only regret was that Tysen was a victim of war – and not by my hand. Well, the others, all the rest is history. It was easy to be out of town on my job and sneak back. I really liked Bill, too," Tom said wistfully.

"So you are going to kill me also?" Kit asked quietly.

A car pulled into the yard, and a broad smile crossed his face. "No, I have something better in mind for you. That's a friend of mine. He's going to take you to a place where there's plenty of fat old men that will pay good money to, um, say amuse themselves with you.

"Tyler didn't stop the boys from driving and I want him to suffer. Taking you away from him, he will think you skipped out on him." He grinned again.

"Tyler will never believe that."

"Sure he will when I show him the pictures of us together. None of us ever expected you were so kinky," he said as he slipped out of his jacket and undid his belt. He backed to the door to answer the knock and let in two men. They spoke in hushed tones. "This is your newest addition," Tom motioned toward Kit.

The man looked Kit up and down. "She'll do. Hurry up and do what you want," and he went outside. The second man brought out a camera and nodded to Tom.

"Now you're going to know what it is to have a real man, Kitty Cat. I can't wait for Tyler to see these pictures of us."

"Tyler's going to find you, Tom, and make you pay for this," Kit shouted defiantly as Tom pinned her to the couch.

He held both of her wrists over her head with one hand and with his free hand ripped the sleeve off of her blouse as she thrashed about. The photographer laughed, "Go get her, Tom," as he rapidly took picture after picture.

Kit struggled and screamed. He stopped abruptly. "We can either do this very painfully or with your permission," he chuckled.

Kit was overwhelmed and angry at the same time. "Go to Hell," she seethed.

Tom threw back his head and roared with laughter. "Now, is that a nice thing for a girl like you to say?" He ripped at her slacks with his free hand, still pinioning her arms. He unzipped his trousers. Leering at her, he told the photographer, "Get a closeup of this." He smiled and the photographer came nearer. Tom let go of her arms so he could shift her body. Kit flailed at him as he waited for pictures to be taken. Kit she began to laugh.

"You're such a fool," she shouted. "Tyler's ten times the man you'll ever hope to be."

"You haven't had me yet!"

"Yes, he's the best lover any woman could hope for!"

Tom's anger unleashed, he slapped her across the mouth, his ability to do anything else gone. He shoved her body away from him angrily. "Get dressed, you slut." Putting his own clothes together, he stormed out of the cabin.

Kit used her blouse sleeve to mop up the blood from her split lip and stared icily at the man with the camera. He grinned and nodded his head. "You're going to be hard to handle. That's okay, my employer likes fire."

"Play with fire and you get burned!" Kit retorted.

The man guffawed and left as Tom returned.

Amanda had to run to keep up with the sheriff. The tires squealed as Tyler floored the gas pedal and they headed in the direction Tom had taken Kit.

Tyler called the office for back up cars, giving them the general direction. He chose to take the lake road, but there were so many secluded areas where his brother could kill the woman he loved. The three other deputies all were in the area looking, so if at all possible they would find Kit in time.

"Why are we looking at the lake, Tyler? That darn Porsche of his goes so fast he could be in the next county by now," Amanda shouted over the roar of the engine.

"All of the other deaths involved drownings. My best guess is that he's taken Kit to the lake."

"Mobile 4 to Sheriff Stone," crackled the radio.

Tyler grabbed the radio microphone. "Stone here, over."

"I see some activity at the old Simpson place, Sheriff, over."

"Thanks, Bob. I'm near there now. Stay ready. Out." Tyler shouted to Amanda, "Mobile 4 is the lake patrol boat." He turned on the siren and headed the squad car down Simpson's road.

Amanda dug her fingernails into the palms of her hands. This whole thing seemed the worst nightmare of her life, but the siren assured her of the reality.

Tom and the other two men heard the patrol car's siren at the same time as Kit. She smiled and thanked God that Tyler was coming. Tom's accomplices ran for their dark sedan and drove away.

"Come on, they're ready to leave," Tom ordered as he dragged Kit out the door. She was half naked and stumbling barefoot toward the Porsche. He shoved her into the car as she fought to get away. He stunned her as he backhanded her, gaining enough time to gun the motor and drive straight toward the oncoming siren.

Kit tried again to interfere with his driving and he backhanded her again, knocking her into darkness. He didn't slow down nor move to one side as Tyler appeared but laughed hysterically as he forced the patrol car into the shrubs along the road.

Tom sped away, leaving Tyler to get his patrol car under control and turned around. "Attention all cars. The suspect's vehicle has been spotted heading south toward Lake Road. All cars, be on the lookout for a silver Porsche driving at a high rate of speed. The suspect has a hostage. I repeat, the suspect has a hostage."

"I should let you out here, Amanda," Tyler shouted over the siren, "but, I can't stop. Do you understand?"

"I'm with you, Tyler. Get him before he hurts Kit!"

Another patrol car was at Lake Road intersection and Tom had to veer his car down one of the many dead ends. He saw Kit was coming to and he fished around for the gun. Even if his brother caught him, he would not have his precious Kitty Cat.

Tom looked back to the road too late to stop the Porsche from hitting a tree on his side of the vehicle and then careening over the embankment. Kit didn't have the seatbelt on so she was thrown free of the convertible as the car plunged into the water. Hitting the water hurt and it was difficult to for her to stay afloat.

She heard Tom's screaming somewhere in the background. The impact of the tree had crushed part of the door into the steering column and trapped him. His flailing about only lasted a short time.

The lake patrol boat was there just ahead of the sheriff and one of the deputies jumped in and pulled Kit out of the water. The other deputy threw him a blanket. He wrapped Kit up just as Tyler and Amanda arrived on the run.

"Is she alive?" he called, the anguish evident in his voice. "Kathryn, darling," he crooned and pulled her limp form into his arms.

Kit coughed. "Just shaken up. Oh Tyler."

Amanda put her arms around the two of them. She looked at the deputies. "What about Tom?"

"The driver was trapped behind the wheel, Ma'am. The young lady here was lucky to be thrown out of the car."

"Thank you for everything," she smiled weakly and turned to see Tyler crying and rocking Kit in his arms.

The county prosecutor swooped into Kensington with the sheriff's report of kidnapping and attempted sex slave operation. Both Monica and the librarian turned state's witnesses against the migrant "boss." Monica only entertained the criminals at her restaurant – her crime being that she turned a blind eye to what she knew was going on. The librarian, however, aided the criminals by coordinating the teenagers, that did their bidding, with the boss and with Tom. That information, along with what was learned from Summer and Kit's sleuthing, was enough to bring charges against the migrant bracero boss and his company.

The state commission on drug trafficking had substantial evidence against the group and a lengthy investigation had come to a close at the same time.

Sadly, all the information Kit and Summer had found about the 1990 basketball team members' deaths, plus Tom's confession to Kit, put the lid on the ugly case of Tom's psychotic revenge. Tyler blamed himself for not recognizing the full impact of his brother's anger; but also knew that Tom was an expert at deceit. Tom had been conveniently away on his business trips when Spencer and Gregory were killed. He had come home early when he pushed his uncle to his death. Tom was also able to come into town unseen when he killed Melton and Kit's brother, Bill. He was helped to hide out by the migrant boss in both cases in exchange for being a drug runner on his business trips.

A few days later Kit, Summer, and Amanda stood in the Kensington graveyard with the sheriff. Only this time, Tyler wore a dark suit and was the one saying goodbye to a loved one. He only hoped that the whole experience had not soured Kit on the idea of marriage. He loved her more than his own life.

The mourners drove the short distance back to the church where the women's association had prepared a luncheon. Tyler was speaking to one of his deputies when he overhead a shopkeeper talking with Kit and Summer. "I suppose now that you proved Bill's death was actually a murder you'll be going back home, Kathryn."

Kit smiled slightly and then looked toward Tyler. "It depends on a lot of things."

Summer laughed. "Now that we have the business going strong, she had better not leave!" She saw Tyler walking toward them. "Jake, have you had some of the little cocktail wieners? They're great," She steered the shopkeeper toward the buffet, giving Kit a hidden wink.

Tyler excused himself and made his way toward Kit who had just sat down by Amanda. "May I join two of Kensington's loveliest?"

Amanda smiled and patted the chair next to her, thus putting herself between Tyler and her daughter. "I'm no longer a Kensingtonite, or is it Kensingtonian? No matter, I am going home as soon as you tell me when I am supposed to come back for your wedding."

When neither Kit nor Tyler answered Amanda she looked at both of them and said sternly, "Don't you dare let this sickness ruin your future. What about your faith?" She stood up and stalked toward the buffet.

Kit slid into the empty chair. "She's right. I seem to remember your saying that you don't play games."

"Only once, with you," smiled Tyler, "but I played for keeps."

Kit held her hand to the light and watched the stones on her ring sparkle. She turned and smiled at Tyler. "Then we're both winners, Ty."

About the Author

Laura Taylor Photography

Shirley Swift has lived all of her life within forty miles of the city of her birth, Hartford, Michigan. She has three children and seven grandchildren.

She researched and compiled genealogical and historical information for three non-fiction books, the most recent **"Henderson Castle – Kalamazoo's Legacy 1895-2013"** was released in June of 2013.

"Deadly Game" is her third novel. Watch for **"Jessie's Castle"** a child-friendly historical ghost story.

Books written by Shirley Swift [Howe]:
Van Buren Genealogies, Volume I and Volume II
Legacy of Five Wives
Love Remembered

The author and her son, Ted Howe own
Eastwood Books Publishing and Distribution
They collaborate on short stories that are published on line.

EASTWOOD BOOKS
Publishing & Distributing
1420 Huntington Avenue
Kalamazoo, MI 49048
eastwoodbooks@gmail.com

Made in the USA
Charleston, SC
14 April 2014